MEN OF INKED SINNERS
BOOK 3

Need

www.chellebliss.com

CHELLE BLISS

USA TODAY BESTSELLING AUTHOR

NEED COPYRIGHT © 2025

Publisher © Chelle Bliss June 20, 2025
Edited by Lisa A. Hollett
Proofread by Read By Rose & Shelley Charlton
Cover Design © Chelle Bliss

CHELLE BLISS

CHAPTER 1
LULU

"STUPID CAR." I kick the tire, hating the potholes that never seem to go away and only grow bigger through the winter.

I didn't even see the damn thing in the middle of the road before my entire brain was jarred from the impact and my tire popped like it was a flimsy balloon.

I bend down, staring at the damaged rim. "Damn it."

This isn't going to be a simple change-the-tire job that I could do myself. I really don't have time to deal with this today. I have a meeting with a new client in two hours to go over the whole-house organization package she purchased from me yesterday. Business has really started to take off lately, especially since I began posting my work on social media more consistently.

I grab my phone from the passenger seat and dial the number for roadside assistance. The woman on the other end tells me someone will be to me within a half hour.

> **Me:** My tire's blown.

> **Tate:** Oh no. Want me to come get you?

The last thing I want is for Tate to come rescue me. She is a new mom and has bigger responsibilities than bailing me out for a stupid tire.

> **Me:** No. Roadside is on the way.

> **Nino:** What happened?

> **Me:** Pothole.

> **Mason:** Hate them. It's why I won't get a car.

He's full of it. The boy is cheap, and he hates parting with his money for just about everything, including a car, gas, and insurance.

> **Amelia:** At least your heater still works.

I crank it up as soon as I read her message, thankful that the car is still running since it's barely above freezing today.

Spring can't come soon enough. I'm not a winter girl, no matter how cute some of the clothes are.

> **Zoey:** Lemme know where you're headed, and I'll pick you up.

> **Me:** Can I borrow your car for the day?

> **Zoey:** Sure thing. I'm working at the bar later.

> **Brax:** I'll give you a ride home after work.

I love my family. Sure, they are a pain in the ass sometimes, but they are the absolute best. Doesn't matter what kind of shit I get myself into, someone always has my back.

> **Me:** Thanks, cousin.

> **Tate:** Let us know when the tow is there.

> **Me:** Will do.

I close the group chat and open my favorite app, reading through comments on my latest posts about my last job, which was a home office redo.

Each video reaches a bigger audience, and although I still have a small following, it's no less exciting to see it grow.

I lose track of time on the side of the highway, trying to ignore the cars whizzing by me at such a fast speed that they could demolish my car with a mere swipe of the side.

Don't think about it, Lulu. You'll be fine. You're not going to die today.

I glance up as the rumble of a diesel engine hits my ears. The tow truck pulls in front of me and slowly backs up, stopping a good ten feet away.

Put a smile on your face.

I've been told I have a solid resting bitch face, and I need to remind myself to smile when I'm hoping someone else doesn't treat me like crap. Not just any someone, but men. Women never care if I'm smiling or wearing a scowl, but any other facial expression seems to set most men on edge. Fragile egos.

I climb out of the car as the tow door opens, and a man steps out who looks big enough to block out the sun. "Ma'am," he says in the deepest, gravelly voice.

I crane my neck upward, following his torso until I can get a good look at his face. "Sir," I reply, always hating being called ma'am. I'm not old enough for that shit, but I'm more than willing to throw it back at them, hoping it rubs them the wrong way too.

The sunshine is almost blinding, and I have to shade my eyes with my hands to be able to focus on his face.

Damn. He's a stunner. He looks like he hiked

down the mountain this morning after chopping a pile of wood and started a fire by rubbing two sticks together to keep warm while he sipped on his black coffee. My mouth instantly waters at the fullness of his lips, which are still visible even though his beard is thick and dark.

"Where's the issue?"

I point toward the front passenger side, unable to move from behind my door. My eyes follow his movement, soaking in his hotness.

I hate winter clothes. I can't tell what his body looks like underneath his heavy coat, and I sure as hell can't see his ass because the coat is too long.

"That's going to need a tow."

I don't dare mutter *duh*, but it's on my lips. It's why I called him. "Oh no," I say, playing the stupid woman act, hoping it'll get this entire ordeal over quicker.

"Why don't you give me the keys and hop up in the truck to stay warm. No need for both of us to freeze to death."

"Keys are in the car," I tell him. "Lemme grab my things." I bend over, reaching across the front seat to snag my purse and phone. I glance through the windshield, and our eyes lock.

The air rushes from my lungs as I soak in his piercing blue eyes. Is there anything about this man that isn't good? Maybe he has nasty teeth, and it'll instantly ruin any fantasy I'm building with him in my mind.

"Act normal," I tell myself as I pull my upper body out of my car. "Don't embarrass yourself, Lulu."

I keep my eyes forward, not looking over at him as I start to walk toward the passenger side of the tow truck. I'm doing my best to walk and not fall in the snow when I hear the man yell, "Watch out."

Suddenly, I'm tumbling into the snow with a heavy weight on top of me and the loudest crash I'd ever heard in my life ringing in my ears.

When I come to a stop, I'm on my back and looking up into the eyes of the hot, burly guy. "Are you okay?" he asks, his eyes searching mine as he breathes heavily, panic written all over his face.

"What happened?" I whisper, unable to speak any louder with the weight of his body crushing me, but I'm not about to complain. This is more action than I've had in months.

Our mouths are a few inches apart, so close I can feel his warm, minty breath against my face. "A car hit yours."

I glance to the side where my car is—or, I should say, was. "Fuck," I groan, slamming my head back into the snow, and squeeze my eyes shut.

If my day was bad before, it just got worse.

"Are you hurt?" the burly tow truck driver asks me again.

"I don't think so." But that doesn't mean tomorrow I won't feel the tumble I've just taken against my will deep down in my muscles.

"Fuck. That was close," he mutters.

Then it hits me. I was standing right where the car must've sideswiped mine, missing his tow truck, but sending my car off into the woods on the side of the highway.

"You saved me," I breathe, my fingers touching his jeans near his ass somewhere.

"I couldn't let you die."

"You could've," I argue.

This handsome man stares down at me and, with a straight face, says, "Darlin', what kind of man would I be if I let you die right in front of my eyes if I could save your life?"

"One who had an overwhelming sense of self-preservation," I tell him.

Would I have done the same? I'm a good person, but I don't know if I could literally jump toward a moving car to save a stranger, even a hot one.

He smirks at my statement as he pushes himself off me and then holds out a hand to me.

I don't hesitate in taking his hand and being pulled up from the ground like I weigh nothing.

God, I love strong men. Smart is a bonus, but strong…that gets my motor running. Maybe that will change as I get older, but for right now, it is high up there on the list of important qualities I want in a man. Is it stupid? Probably, but I don't give a crap.

When my eyes move to where my car used to be, I suck in a breath as the realization crashes over me. A minute earlier and I would've been bending over, half inside, half outside, to grab my purse. A few minutes before that and I would've been completely inside, waiting for the lumberjack tow truck driver to get here.

"Don't worry," the guy says at my side, "I have a dashcam. We'll find out who that asshole was."

I hadn't even realized the person never stopped after demolishing my car like he meant to do it. "Damn," I mutter, shaking my head. "Why would they leave?"

"A bunch of reasons. Maybe they were drunk or had an outstanding warrant."

"Asshole," I whisper and turn my gaze toward Mr. Burly. "Not you. Them." I fling my arm out toward the pieces of my car that stayed where the entire thing used to be.

He reaches into his pocket, fishing out his phone. "That they are, darlin'. I'll call this in."

"Call it in?" I ask, totally missing that he said darlin'. Any other time, those words would've made my belly flutter, but right now, I am knee-deep in shock to feel much of anything.

"The police."

I nod as he lifts the phone to his ear. "Right," I

mutter, and I am happy at least one of us is thinking clearly.

I turn my body, staring out across the highway, and watch the cars move past in a blur. I've never been that close to dying before. If he hadn't tackled me, I wouldn't be breathing right now. It all happened in the blink of an eye, and that is the scariest part of it. One minute, you're here, and the next… you're not.

"They're on the way."

"Thanks," I say, my voice soft compared to the buzz of the traffic.

The man touches my back so gently, I almost don't feel it. "Why don't we wait in the truck. It's not safe to stand here."

I can't argue with him. His point was proven a few minutes ago. "Okay," I say, sounding more like a zombie than myself.

My feet move on their own, trusting this man with every fiber of my being. He guides me toward the passenger door of his giant tow truck, which looks more like a tank compared to my cute little sports car.

"Up you go," he says after opening the door for me and moving his hand from my back to my arm. "You'll be safer in here."

"Yeah," I whisper, grabbing the bar inside the truck to haul myself up. I'm not short, but this truck makes me feel dainty and little.

As soon as I'm situated, staring straight ahead, he

closes the door and walks around the truck, talking to himself.

As much as this is a pain for me, I'm sure he didn't have this on his bingo card today. What was supposed to be a simple job has now made him into a witness to a crime.

"I called my partner to tow your car out of the woods," he says as he settles into the seat next to me. "His truck is built better for going off-road."

"Thanks," I say again, but I don't think I can say it enough. There's so much to thank him for, specifically me still being alive.

"You wet?" he asks.

I snap my head to the side, and my eyes widen. "What?"

"Are you wet?" he asks again.

I blink a few times in even more shock than I was when I almost died. "Excuse me?" I finally ask.

"From the snow," he explains, looking at me like I have three eyes.

"Oh," I whisper, feeling like an idiot. "Yes." I've been in such shock, I didn't even realize my entire backside is covered in snow. It didn't begin to melt until I climbed into the warmth of his truck. "I'm sorry about your seat."

"Darlin', that seat's been through more than a little water." He smiles at me as he reaches for the knob to adjust the temperature. "It's seen some things."

I grimace, but I don't ask him what some things are because I don't want to know. I lift my hands toward the vents, closing my eyes as the heat moves over my skin.

"I'll handle the cops when they get here."

"Okay."

"Hey," he says in a firm voice, "Look at me."

I swing my gaze his way because something about his tone makes it impossible for me not to.

"You *are* safe. It's all going to be okay."

I may be okay, but based on the hunk of metal I saw near the woods, my car is not. I guess I'll be spending the weekend car shopping because I have to be able to get to my client meetings. "I know."

He lifts an eyebrow above his beautiful blue eyes. "Do you?"

I nod. "I almost just died, but I'm alive."

"Yes," he says back, smiling.

"I'll snap out of it," I promise him.

"You don't need to snap out of it but settle into it. Realize you got lucky, but don't take too long."

"I've settled into it. I was just thinking about having to go look at new cars." I skip over the bit about getting lucky. I wouldn't have been if he hadn't been there. I'd be just as mangled as my car.

"Good," he says.

It's my turn to raise an eyebrow. "When is car shopping good? It's a nightmare. I'd rather stick toothpicks under my fingernails than talk to a car salesman."

He barks out a laugh. "Your words are colorful."

"Do you like car shopping?"

His headshake is immediate. "Lucky for me, my stepdad is a car salesman. I call him, and he makes it happen without all the bullshit."

"Can he make it happen for me too?" I ask, wishing the guy could work more miracles in my life, like sparing me from the wheeling and dealing I hate so much. It always feels like a scam to rip people off.

"Sure," he says, surprising me.

I take a moment to finally look over his features and study his face. The last so many minutes have been a whirlwind of excitement that I don't want to repeat anytime soon.

The city lumberjack is more handsome than I first noticed. Maybe it's because of everything that just happened, but his eyes are even more stunning than they were outside. His beard is thicker than I thought but isn't unruly. The man spends time on it to make it look good. His lips are full and lush, made to spend hours kissing someone.

"Sure?" I ask, wondering if I heard him wrong.

He nods, giving me a glimpse of his straight white teeth. "Randall is always looking for business."

"I already owe you so much for saving my life, but I'm going to owe you even more if you make car-buying painless."

"You owe me nothing, darlin'. I was in the right place at the right time."

It feels like it is more than that. I'm not sure many people would put their own lives at risk to save a stranger, but he did it without a second thought.

"Cop's here," he says, reaching for his door handle. "Stay put. I've got you."

And for the first time in my life, I think a man finally does.

CHAPTER 2
OLIVER

LIAM STEPS out of his truck, and his eyes go straight to the wreck a good thirty feet off the side of the highway where the cop is taking notes. Her car's a pile of shit, smashed against a bank of trees. "Well, shit," he mutters, running his hand back and forth over the top of his head. "This is gonna be a bitch."

The temperature has risen throughout the day, and the sunshine that finally decided to make an appearance is doing a number on the snow covering the ground. My truck would get stuck in the mud before I'd make it halfway to its destination, but I figured Liam's could do it without an issue.

"Should I call someone else?" I ask him as the cop walks our way with his fancy clipboard and my driver's license that I'd given him when he first arrived.

"Nah, man. I got it. She's lucky she wasn't in it,"

he says as he ticks his chin toward the back of the woman's head while she waits in the cab of my truck.

"She was outside of it, but I got her out of the way."

Liam's eyes widen. "Are you crazy?"

I shrug. "Was I supposed to watch her die?"

"No, but damn, Oli. Ma would've lost her shit if you'd gone off and gotten yourself killed."

My brother. He's so poetic with his words.

"Sir, here's your license back and hers," the cop says, handing me everything, including her stuff. "If you could have her come down to the station on South Halstead to give a statement and drop off the dashcam footage before the end of the day, we'd appreciate it."

"Will do," I tell him, stashing our stuff in my side jacket pocket.

"Sir," the cop says, tipping his head toward my brother.

"Officer," Liam says through his teeth, hiding his sneer behind his unkempt beard.

Liam's never been a fan of law enforcement, especially in the city. He spent way too much time with them as a teenager because he was always doing dumb shit and getting caught. Despite his best efforts, he didn't have the smarts for a life of crime.

Liam's eyes are trained on the cop as he walks back toward his cruiser. "I'm surprised they even bothered showing up."

"Hit-and-run always gets their blood pumping."

"They do love to arrest people," he says, and he'd know. I've never been arrested in my life, but my brother…he has a frequent customer card with the county jail.

"You got this?" I ask, glancing toward my truck and the pretty girl tucked inside.

"Yup," he snaps. "You got her?"

I nod. "Always."

"She hot?"

"Yeah. She's way too pretty for you, man."

"Bullshit," he mutters. "No such thing."

My brother is good-looking, and boy, oh boy, does he know it. But he has a knack for ruining sweet things like her. He sucks them in and quickly turns their world upside down, leaving them a bigger mess than her smashed-up car. I won't let that happen with her. She's too nice for that…too sweet.

"She's mine, Liam."

His eyebrows shoot up as he pulls his head back. "She's what?"

"Off-limits to you, buddy," I tell him as I step backward, making my way back to where she's waiting.

"Yeah. Yeah," he says, swiping his hand in the air to brush me off. "I got my hands full with Sharla anyway. Don't need to add another to the roster."

Sharla. She is something. Very pretty, but a little off her rocker. Exactly the way Liam prefers his women. Stable and sane are not words to describe any of his long-term girlfriends. He met Sharla at the Pink Flamingo as she shook her moneymaker on the stage in front of him and still does three nights a week.

"Catch ya later," I call out as I get to my truck door, wanting to get inside the warm cabin because the wind is wicked today, and there's a good-smelling pretty thing waiting for me too.

"Bye!" he yells back before I climb inside.

"Everything okay?" she asks, her big brown eyes still filled with so much worry.

"All good," I tell her, fishing the shit the cop gave me out of my side pocket. "You gotta go down to the station today and make a statement."

"I didn't see anything," she says as she grabs her license from my hand.

"Just tell them what you did see and what you know. The dashcam and my statement will fill in the rest."

She tips her head back against the seat. "I can do that," she says with a sigh. "I'll have to get a ride."

"We can go now if you want," I offer, for no good reason.

I want to stick close to her, and I don't know why. I've met plenty of pretty women before. Hell, I've spent way too many nights with them too, but there is something about this one and the state of shock she is in that have me wanting to stick around.

"I'm sure you have better things to do than hang out with me."

"Not really," I answer honestly. Sure, I could be working, but with the wind and cold, I'd do almost anything to get out of being outdoors right now. And being around her isn't a hardship. I can't think of a better way to spend my day. "I have to go down there too so they can get a copy of my dashcam video."

"I canceled my meeting with my client already, so I'm free if you are."

"Free as a bird," I tell her, putting the truck in drive. "Buckle up."

Without hesitating, she does as she's told. I don't know if she's always this easy or if she's still in shock over what happened.

"You need a ride home after the station?" I ask her, because why the hell not. I'll do whatever to spend more time with her and not just because anything beats freezing my ass off in the cold.

"I can get a ride."

"Darlin', I have a truck and some time. You want a ride home after the station?"

"Sure," she says, picking up her phone when the screen lights up. "But I hate to put you out."

"You're not putting me out. I offered."

"Okay, but only if you let me buy you lunch."

I glance her way, wondering if I heard her right. "Lunch?"

She gives me a smile that makes me warmer than

the sun ever has on a summer day. "My family owns a place, and they make the best burgers in town."

"I'm not one to ever turn down a good burger," I say, but the woman could've offered me anything and I would've jumped at a chance to spend more time with her.

"The best. I said the best, not good."

"So, you said client. What do you do for work?" I ask, making the question seem like small talk, but really, I'm gathering intel. I have an overwhelming need to know everything about her. I know the basics from her license, but besides the events of earlier, I don't know much else.

"I'm an organizer."

I've heard of some crazy-ass ideas to make money, but never in my life have I heard someone say they're an organizer. "Like a maid?"

"No. I suck at cleaning," she says, staring down at her phone screen again, tapping away at the glass. "I take what they have and make it accessible and easy to use. I declutter their life a bit and make sure everything has a proper place."

"People pay you for that?" I ask, and it comes out harsh and judgmental. But obviously, I'm not rich enough to understand paying someone to move my shit around my place.

"Yeah, and they pay well."

"Huh. Well, I'll be damned," I mutter. "You must be good."

"I'm the best in the city."

"I wouldn't say my place is organized, but I know where everything is when I need it."

"Then you're organized."

"The garage isn't, though, but that's because my brother never puts anything back where it should go."

"You want some help with that?" she asks, making me glance her way again.

"I don't think I could afford you." Her car had been cute but pricey, and her clothes aren't giving me thrift-store vibes. The woman is classy and way out of my league, but that doesn't stop me from going out of my way to spend more time with her.

"I'll give you a helluva discount for saving my life and helping me get a new car."

I forgot about that. I'll have to beg Randall to give the girl the family discount and not screw her over like he usually does with his other customers. "It's a deal," I tell her, but then it hits me. Liam will be at the garage, and he's the last person I want around her. Sharla or no, the man loves women, especially pretty little things like her.

"I have some time week after next in the evening."

Liam's on vacation soon. He and Sharla are going to Vegas to party it up like they don't do that every day here in the city. It's just an excuse to drink and gamble nonstop without anyone thinking they're lushes or degenerates. Vegas has a way of making everything that's bad somehow look good.

"That'll work."

"Perfect," she says, tapping away on the screen again, "What's the garage's name so I can put it in my phone?"

"Winston Brothers."

"Got it," she says as I ease onto Halstead near the station. "It should only take a few days."

"You haven't seen the garage."

"You haven't seen my skills."

God, I like her attitude. Unlike after the accident when she was a jumble of emotions and a hot mess, when she talks about her work, she's confident and self-assured.

"I'm Oliver, but my friends call me Oli."

"I like that," she says. "I'm Lulu, and sometimes people call me Lou."

"Lou," I whisper her name, and I like the way it sounds on my lips.

"Here we are," I tell her as I stop in front of the station, taking a spot on the street to avoid paying the ridiculous prices to park in a city lot. "You still good with doing this now?"

"As good as I'll ever be, but I don't remember anything besides you on top of me."

I remember it too, and I haven't been able to think of much else on the entire ride to the station. There is something about this chick that sticks under my skin and has my mind wandering to all the possibilities that will never become reality.

"I don't think they need to know about that," I tell her, killing the engine of the truck.

Her eyes meet mine, and for a moment, I can't breathe. "But you're a hero," she says with so much seriousness, it makes my chest squeeze a little bit.

"I don't think anyone's ever called me that before. I was just in the right place at the right time."

"You need to be nicer to yourself. You did something good, Oli."

It's not lost on me that she called me Oli and not Oliver. "Anyone would've done it, Lou."

She smiles when I use her nickname. "That's not true," she says as she turns her gaze toward the brick building at our side. "I'm ready to get this over with because I'm starving and want that burger. You ready?"

"Let's do it, darlin'," I tell her as I reach for the door handle when she does.

I climb out, watching her as she slides out of my truck instead of hopping down. I shake my head as I round the front to meet her on the sidewalk.

It only takes a few minutes before we're put into a private room, and an officer sits down with us to take our statements. As Lou talks, I search through the dashcam files from today, finding the one they'll need.

"I found the video," I tell the cop as I set my phone down on the table.

Lou's eyes move to the screen. "Can I see it?"

"Sure," I tell her, pushing my phone in front of her, and tap on the screen.

I didn't watch the whole thing before I pressed play. I don't know how much or how little information they'll be able to get off the clip. Hopefully the camera worked today because sometimes it is more temperamental than my mother, and that is saying something.

I stare at Lou's profile as her gaze is pinned on the video. She's truly beautiful, with high cheekbones, a straight nose, and big brown eyes that might very well be able to see straight into my soul. She chews on her lips as she watches the video, and I wonder how soft they are and if she's a good kisser.

"Oh my God," she says, her hand flying to her mouth. "You were so close to being hit."

My gaze drops to the phone as she slides her finger across the screen to replay the last few seconds, the entire reason we're here. I watch the video this time too instead of staring at her, and it's not lost on me how very close we both came to dying today.

"You were the one who was close," I tell her, unable to take my eyes off the car in the video as it hauls ass in her direction like she was the target.

Lou reaches out, placing her small hand on my arm, curling it around my jacket. "Oliver, you literally jumped in front of me as you pushed me down. The car was inches away from you."

"And you," I remind her because I'm not the only one who had a brush with death.

"That was a very heroic act," the officer says as her eyes move away from my phone screen and back to the stack of paperwork in front of her. "We don't see that very often."

"Right?" Lou says to the female officer. "He could've let me die."

"Never," I grumble. I'm not built like that. "I didn't even think about it. I just reacted."

Lou's hand tightens around my arm. "I owe you more than a burger, Oliver."

"You're going to organize the garage," I remind her of the other part of her thank-you gift. I couldn't care less about her moving shit around. I just want to spend more time with her.

"I don't think I'll ever be able to repay you."

"There's nothing to repay, Lou."

She turns her eyes toward me and gives me a smile that barely reaches her high cheekbones. "There is, though."

"I have to agree with her," the cop says, like it's any of her business. I wasn't looking for her input, even if it is nice to hear.

"See?" Lou says, lifting her other hand toward the lady across the table from us. "Everyone will agree with me. When I tell my family…"

"Don't tell anyone. It's not a big deal," I say to

her. I've never been comfortable with praise, even when it's deserved.

"Oh hush," she says to me, and for some odd reason, my cock jerks in my pants.

Fuck. Why does this girl get to me? She's so bossy and doesn't give a crap that I'm easily twice her size.

The officer chuckles as she pushes some paperwork in front of Lou. "If you could please just read over the statement and sign at the bottom, Ms. Gallo, we can get this wrapped up."

"And Mr. Winston, if you could email that clip to the address on my card and sign your portion of the statement, we'll be all set."

"Not a problem," I tell her, taking the phone from in front of Lou, who's been playing the part where I tackle her on repeat since she first saw it. It has to be burned into her brain now.

"We'll see if we can pull a plate or something off the video, and we'll be in touch if we need anything else from either of you," the officer says.

"Okay," Lou replies, pulling her hand away from my arm to hold the paper in place so she can sign it.

"I'm here for whatever you need," I tell the lady cop. "Assholes like that shouldn't be on the road."

"Agreed," she says, giving me a smile, "But as long as there are good guys like you out there, the world shakes out in the end."

Good guys. It's almost laughable. I'm not a bad

one. I'm not my brother Liam. But good? I don't know about that.

After Lou is finished signing, she slides the papers my way, and I riffle through the stack until I get to my statement, which is a little longer than hers. I scribble my name on the line marked "witness," and everything I can do to catch the guy is done on my end and hers.

"Do you need to call anyone?" the woman asks Lou as I push the stack of papers back in her direction.

"No, I'm taking Oliver to lunch. He'll give me a ride."

My mind instantly goes places it shouldn't. Me on top of her, but instead of layers of winter clothes in a pile of snow, we're in my bed and both gloriously naked.

"You ready to eat?" Lou asks me.

In my mind, I already am, but instead of a burger, I'm feasting on the taste of her sweet skin. "Yeah."

"Thanks for coming in so quickly," the cop says. "Hopefully we catch the guy."

"I won't hold my breath," I mumble because although the Chicago cops love arresting people, they're shit at finding hit-and-run drivers, no matter how hard they try.

Lou's hands drop to her stomach. "I need food before I get hangry."

I smile at her, wondering how hangry she gets and

what that looks like. I can't imagine her as anything other than this sweet and sometimes emotionally messy girl beside me.

"Let's get you fed," I tell her as I slide the chair back and stand, holding out my hand to her.

"I promise it'll be the best thing you'll ever put in your mouth," she says to me as she places her palm in mine and pushes herself upward off the chair.

"We'll see about that," I tell her, but my mind isn't thinking about a burger.

CHAPTER 3
LOU

"WHAT?" my dad asks as he throws a towel over his shoulder, standing above our table and staring at me like I've grown an extra head.

Of course, he had to be working this afternoon. He would find out about the accident sooner or later, but I was definitely hoping it was later.

I motion toward Oliver, who looks like he's a deer in headlights. The man jumped in front of a speeding car, but he suddenly looks petrified in front of my dad.

"Dad, I'm fine. It's no big deal."

Dad drops into the open chair at my side and takes my hand in his. "You could've died."

"But I didn't," I tell him, turning my head toward Oliver. "He made sure of that."

"I don't know how to thank you," Dad says to

Oliver, who's squirming in his seat like he's sitting in a puddle.

"No thanks needed. I'm happy I was there to help."

"Help?" Dad's eyes are wide and wild, a look I know well when he's panicked. "Help is changing a tire, not saving someone's life."

"Hey. Hey," Aunt Daphne says, walking into the bar in the cutest pair of black leather boots that almost kiss the hem of her knee-length skirt. "What's up?"

Dad doesn't even look in her direction when he says, "Lou almost died today."

Aunt Daphne stops mid-step, her one foot still in the air. "What?"

"Her car broke down, and she was on the side of the road when another car came speeding at her, but this guy—" Dad throws a hand toward Oliver "—pushed her out of the way before it could hit her."

Aunt Daphne gasps, covering her mouth as she finally stands on two feet. "Damn," she whispers into her palm. "That's some crazy shit. You okay, kiddo?"

I nod and drag my gaze toward Oliver, who's still sitting silently, staring straight at me. "Help," he mouths, and I giggle softly.

"What's so funny? Is dying funny?" Dad asks, and I suddenly feel like a little kid again, being chastised for some stupid thing my cousins talked me into doing.

"No, Dad. Dying isn't funny at all," I tell him, not looking in his direction because I don't want to see the all-too-familiar look that goes along with his tone.

"Who's the hunk?" Aunt Daphne asks, and I can't stop the smile from forming on my lips.

Dad grumbles a slew of curse words.

"He's Oliver, the tow truck driver," I answer.

"Well, Oliver, the tow truck driver, thanks for saving my niece. You saved this family a bunch of sadness today."

"Not a problem," Oliver says and shifts his weight again in the wooden chair that's probably too small for his wide frame and that ass I still haven't been able to get a good look at.

"We owe you," Aunt D says to him as she moves toward the bar and sloughs off her coat. "Big-time."

Oliver shakes his head. "The best burger in town is payment enough."

"And I'm going to organize his garage."

"Jesus," Dad mumbles, scrubbing his hand up and down his face in distress. "You're talking like nothing big happened today."

"I've had time to deal with everything, Dad."

"She lost her shit for a while," Oliver adds, "but I made sure she was okay and wasn't in shock too long."

Dad's head swivels toward Oliver. "Thank you. Did I say that already? If not, thank you."

Dad is obviously in shock right now, much like I was earlier.

"You have, and again, no thanks needed."

"What are we thanking him for?" Gram asks, walking out of the back room of the bar.

Jesus. Doesn't anyone in the family have anything else to do today than be here?

"Lou almost got killed today," Aunt Daphne says, so casually my grandma takes a minute to absorb the information and almost stumbles forward.

"What?" Gram screeches.

I roll my eyes. "I'm fine. I'm fine," I reassure her. "He made sure of it."

Oliver's eyes flash, and I know he's sick of hearing the praise, but I'll never stop telling people.

Gram crosses the room, stopping at Oliver's side. "You saved my baby?"

Oliver turns his head upward, still looking nervous. "Yes, ma'am," he tells her.

Gram throws her arms around the man and snuggles into him. "Thank you."

Oliver's almost frozen, and all uncomfortable movement from earlier disappears. "Not a problem," he says as he pats my gram's arm.

"I need to cook for you," Gram says as she backs away, but she keeps her arms on his shoulders. "You deserve so much thanks."

"No, Gram. I'm treating him," I tell her. I don't have the heart to say eating her cooking isn't a thank-you. It's the complete opposite—except for her eggplant parm, which is the best I've ever had. "We're having some burgers."

Gram shakes her head. "A burger doesn't seem like thanks enough."

"It's plenty, ma'am," Oliver tells her, trying to force a smile onto his face.

"Gram," Gram corrects him, and I chuckle.

The scared look on his face doesn't fade. "Um," he mumbles, staring up at her in sheer terror.

"You guys are all over the top," I say. I knew coming here would be a mistake, but I still suggested it. "Stop scaring the man."

"The man jumped in front of a car. I don't think a few people are going to scare him," Dad says.

"You jumped in front of a car?" Gram asks, still touching him. "Oh my word." Gram looks over at me and gives me a look that totally says marry him. "I'll make the burger. You deserve a good meal."

"I've got it," Daphne says, saving us all from my grandmother's cooking. "We do have a cook, Ma."

"But it should be made with love," Gram tells my aunt.

"Not if we want him to keep breathing," Aunt Daphne says as she heads to the kitchen before my grandmother can shoot back a response and argue about her cooking.

Gram's phone rings inside her purse. "Shit. I have to go. I'm meeting the girls for coffee to gossip, and they're going to eat this story up when I tell them about this fine drink of water." She pats Oliver's shoulder, giving him a wink. "You take care of yourself, handsome."

"Thanks," he says, but his voice turns up at the end.

"Don't mind her," I tell him when she runs out of the bar like her ass is on fire. "She can be a bit much."

"A bit?" Dad says, finally laughing.

"Leave the kids alone, Lucio. They need time to talk and decompress. Stop hovering," Aunt Daphne says when she walks back into the bar from the kitchen. "They'll be out in five."

I give her a smile because I'm starving and because she's trying to save us from my father. "Thanks, Auntie."

"Fine," Dad grumbles as he taps the table, completely irritated. "We'll talk about this later."

"Yay, me," I say, earning myself a side-eye glare before he stalks away. "Sorry about that."

"It's okay," Oliver says as his shoulders finally relax and we're alone—or as close as we can be with my dad and aunt still nearby. "They seem nice."

"Seem is the operative word." I smile as my gaze wanders to where my aunt and dad are talking near the bar. "They can be a lot sometimes, even to me, and I was born into this circus."

"Is your family big?"

"Yeah."

"Close?"

"Too much."

Oliver smiles, and my heart flutters in my chest. "That's nice."

"Yours?"

"Small and not close, besides my parents. Everyone else lives out of state."

"Where?" I ask.

"Georgia."

Now the darlin' makes complete sense. "Half of my family lives in Florida, but they moved away before I was born."

"I was around seven when we moved here. My stepdad thought he'd make more money in the big city than the sticks."

"And did he?"

"Yep, and I'm thankful he made that decision every day of my life. I'm not a country boy."

"You look like one," I blurt out, unable to stop myself and my big mouth.

He chuckles. "I like hiking and being outdoors, but I wasn't made to live in the middle of nowhere with nothing to do other than go to church or sit at the local bar. No offense."

"None taken," I say, smiling. "I love the city too. I wasn't made for the outhouse life."

Oliver chuckles loudly, and the sound of it makes my insides warm. He's handsome all the time, but there's something extra special about him when he's laughing. "They have indoor plumbing, Lou."

"Hiking is my limit."

"Camping?" he asks.

I tilt my head, trying to think about the last time I went camping, and I draw a blank. "I don't know if I've ever been. I don't know if I'd survive."

"You got to do it right, and then it's the best thing in the world. Just you and nature."

Now, it's my turn to stare at someone like they have an extra head. "That doesn't sound delightful."

"It is if you do it like I do."

I can almost guarantee if I did anything like he did, I would die from exhaustion and lack of strength. But that doesn't mean my interest isn't piqued. "And how do you do it?"

"A good tent, an air mattress, a roaring fire, some whiskey, and a sky full of stars."

The only time I get a good look at the night sky is when I visit my family in Florida. The Chicago skyline is too bright to see much of anything except the brightest stars.

"I'm going in a couple weeks to see the meteor shower."

"I've never seen one of those. I've heard they're amazing."

"You should come," he says, so casually I don't think he means it.

"Someday."

"This time."

"You're serious?" I ask, leaning forward. "You're asking me to go?"

"Why wouldn't I want you to? I'd love to add pretty girl to the list of how I camp."

My heart does that weird flutter thing inside my chest again. "Can we do s'mores?" I raise an eyebrow, figuring that will be the deal-breaker. I'm giving him a way out if he isn't serious.

"We can do anything you want."

Gah. I want to jump this man's bones, which is so unlike me. I don't know if it's because I'm ovulating or because he saved my life, but the pull is so strong, it is becoming too hard to ignore. "It's kind of cold to camp."

"I'm going south and chasing the heat."

"You sure you don't want to take your wife?" Man, I am fishing for information, and I pray he doesn't realize it.

"Don't got one."

"Girlfriend?"

He shakes his head and smirks. "Just me."

Shit. He knows I was fishing for information, but I guess it doesn't matter. "Let's see how next week goes, and then I'll let you know."

"Just tell me if I should pack for the bike or my other truck."

"Bike?" I ask, both of my eyebrows shooting upward.

"Yeah. I don't get to take her out much this time of year."

"I'm sure."

"But if you come, we can probably haul her with us if you like to ride."

"I love to ride," I tell him, but I'm not sure if I'm talking about his bike anymore—or him.

It's as if the universe plucked my list for a perfect man right out of the sky and put him directly in my path on purpose.

"Then that's what we'll do."

I stare at him, blinking a few times. Is he serious? He can't be. I'm a stranger, and he's suddenly inviting me on a trip deep into the woods with no one else around us. Usually, I would say no. There's no way I'd do that with most men I know, especially one I just met. But this is Oliver, my lumberjack savior, and he literally just saved my life. He wouldn't take me out there to kill me after all the trouble he's been through today, right?

"What are we doing?" Aunt Daphne asks as she sets down two plates with the most beautiful burgers. "Making plans?"

"We're going camping," Oliver says to her as he turns the plate around, putting the burger side toward him instead of the fries.

Aunt D sucks in air between her teeth. "Sounds awful."

Oliver's gaze dips to her boots. "You don't look like the hiking type."

"Not a day in my life. And this one——" Aunt D shoots a look toward me "——isn't much better."

"Noted," Oliver tells her with a smile. "But I'll make sure she's safe."

"I have no doubt," Aunt D tells him before taking a few steps away and glancing over her shoulder, giving me a wink. "Hot," she mouths at me.

"Now, everyone's going to know," I tell him as I grab the ketchup. "And I mean everyone."

"They can come too," he says as he grabs the burger with one hand like it's not half the size of my head.

A pang of sadness washes over me. Was I reading too much into it? Maybe it is just a friends-type trip, even though we aren't even that yet. "Oh no. If you think those three were too much, my cousins are worse."

"If they're all like you, I'll like them," he says before taking the biggest bite I've ever seen.

I imagine his mouth, open that wide, eating something else, and I need to reach for my soda, chugging it like my insides are on fire and need to be cooled.

"You okay?" he asks after he swallows.

"Fine. Fine," I lie as every little nerve ending in my body is screaming at me to touch him or rub my body on him like I'm a cat in heat.

He takes another bite of his burger and groans, closing his eyes as he chews. My fingers curl, my nails digging into the old wood of the tabletop. Damn it. Why am I reacting this way—and in my family's bar, no less? I've seen a man eat before, but it was nowhere near as erotic of an experience.

When Oliver opens his eyes, they land on me. I jolt in my chair, my hands flying to my burger because I need to put food in my mouth to stop myself from saying something completely embarrassing.

"So good," I say around a mouthful of burger.

Oliver nods, jamming a few fries into his mouth. They're great too. The fresh-cut ones that have crispy bits on the ends of the skinny fries. I could eat an entire plate of them with a side of cheese sauce every day of my life and never get sick of them.

When my gaze moves over Oliver's shoulder, Aunt Daphne and Dad are staring at us.

Oh boy. This isn't good.

I'm sure she opened her mouth and told him about the upcoming and unplanned camping trip. I'll hear about this later, but what can Dad say? He can't tell me Oliver is dangerous because the man literally saved my life today.

I can't stop glancing in their direction as I keep eating and trying to carry on a normal conversation with Oliver. Before I have the last bite on my tongue, my mother comes rushing through the front door of the bar.

"Where is she?" Ma says, gasping for air like she ran a marathon, and she frantically glances around the dining room until her eyes land on me.

Great. Dad must've texted her when I wasn't looking and told her everything that happened.

"My baby," Ma says, coming in our direction with her arms open. Before I can react, she has her arms around me, burying my face in her chest. "Thank goodness you're okay." She rocks from side to side, making my stomach turn with its overstuffed contents.

"Ma, please stop."

She only tightens her hold on me. "I don't know what I would've done if something had happened to you."

"Sweetheart," Dad says from nearby, but I can't see anything besides the color of my mother's shirt. "You're strangling her."

"Oh," Ma says, finally releasing me. "I'm sorry. I was just… Who's this?"

I blink a few times as my eyes adjust to the light again. "That's Oliver. He saved me."

"Stop saying that, Lou," Oliver says.

"Lou?" Ma's eyebrows rise as she turns her gaze toward me again.

"He calls you Lou?"

I nod at her. "It's my name."

"Your nickname," she reminds me.

"And if the guy who saved my life can't use it, who should?"

"Right," she says with a curt nod. "How can we repay you?" Ma asks Oliver.

I cover my face with a hand and groan. "Ma."

"What?"

"I have it handled."

"You do?"

I drop my hand into my lap as I stare up at her. "We're starting with a burger."

"And ending with?" she asks, tilting her head with a weird look on her face.

"I'm going to organize his garage."

Her eyebrows draw inward. "You are?"

I nod and reach for a fry. "Uh, yeah. What else would I do?"

She sucks in a breath as she drops into the chair next to me. "I don't know. I don't know what's the right thing when someone saves your life."

"Me either," I tell her as I pop the fry into my mouth. "But I'm going to figure it out."

"Lou, I don't need or want anything," Oliver says for the millionth time.

"Baby," Ma says to him, patting his hand, "you may not need or want something, but you sure as hell deserve it."

Oliver shifts in his seat, forcing a smile on his face. "I did what anyone else would've done in my shoes."

Ma just stares at him, and the look on her face even makes me shift in my seat. "No, they wouldn't.

She knows it. I know it. And you know it." She points her finger at each of us as she speaks.

"You can have burgers on the house for the rest of your life," Dad says to Oliver, and I raise an eyebrow at him.

What is he doing? He's up to something, but I'm not sure what angle he's taking.

"That's too much," Oliver replies.

"Take it," I tell him. "They won't stop until you accept some kind of gift."

Oliver sighs. "Thank you, sir."

Dad's eyes flash because he hates the proper and extremely old terms as much as I do. "You're welcome."

"Can we finish eating?" I ask him and my mom, because we were having a fine time before Mom walked in and lost her mind.

"Sure," Ma says, pushing herself up from her chair as my father takes her hand. "I'll be over there."

"Okay," I tell her, but it's not as if I won't be able to see her. I didn't think she was going to vanish into thin air. As soon as they're back by the bar near Aunt Daphne, I turn my gaze back toward Oliver. "I'm sorry they're so weird."

"I really like them."

"Then you're a weirdo too."

He chuckles as he takes another bite of his burger, which is probably cold since my family can't seem to stop interrupting us.

"So, where are we camping when you say 'down south'?"

"Just outside of Nashville."

My eyes widen. "Really? I've never been to Nashville."

"We'll be outside, but maybe we can go to the city one night."

"How many nights are we going?"

"Four."

I lean back in my chair and try to think about how long four nights is. I mean, I know, but that's with the hustle and bustle of the city, not crickets and wildlife. "I don't know if I can make it four days."

"You can, darlin'."

"I don't think so."

"I know you'll be begging me for more."

CHAPTER 4
OLIVER

LIAM WHISTLES as I stalk into the garage after a cleanup at the local barber. "Lookin' hot, brother."

I give him the middle finger as I round my desk across from his. I don't need his shit today.

"What are you doing tonight? Want to go watch Sharla dance with me?"

I don't even bother looking up from the stack of papers in front of me. "No." I swear he's off his rocker. If he's serious about Sharla at all, why would he want me—her possible future brother-in-law—to watch her dance naked?

"Come on. We can get drunk and look at some tits. I leave for Vegas tomorrow and need to blow off some steam."

"No, and Vegas is how you blow off steam. You don't pre-game a vacation."

He grunts his disapproval. "Does this have

anything to do with that hot piece of ass you've been texting nonstop for the last week?"

Now, I look up, narrowing my eyes. "Do not call her a hot piece of ass."

He rolls his eyes. "Whatever. You're sweet on her. She must have some amazing snatch."

If my glare was hot before, it's now molten. "Watch it, little brother."

He waves his hand at me and laughs. "Totally sweet. I don't think I've ever seen you this flustered over someone."

"I'm not flustered."

"Well, you're something." He grabs his phone and starts typing away on the screen. "How about a movie? They have the newest action one with that guy we like with the accent."

My brother can't remember names and titles to save his life. How in the hell am I supposed to know who he's talking about without any real details besides the accent. "I gotta pass."

"Lulu?" He raises an eyebrow, and I'm shocked he remembers her name.

"Yeah."

"Going out or staying in?"

"Don't know," I tell him, even though I do.

She's coming here at seven, after she finishes with her last client, to look at the garage and figure out how big of a job it'll be.

It's bigger than I think she realizes, but I don't

expect or want her to do much. I agreed to letting her at the shelves and drawers because she begged me, and I think this is the shit she enjoys. I'd do anything to spend a little more time surrounded by her goodness.

"I took Shar to the new joint down the street. Maybe you can go there." His voice sounds genuine, which is a change for him. "They had some killer street tacos."

"I'll remember that."

He places his knuckles on the desk and pushes himself upward. "Well, I'm going to hit it. I promised Shar I'd be there by seven to watch her entire set tonight."

"Cool. Will I see you before you leave tomorrow?"

He shakes his head. "I'm going to roll out of bed and head to Midway, but text me if you need something, and I'll be back in a few days."

"Have fun, and don't get arrested."

He laughs. "I'm way past that part of my life. I'm a law-abiding citizen now."

It's my turn to roll my eyes. "Sure, Li. Whatever you say."

"Enjoy your date tonight. Don't do anything I wouldn't do."

"Is there anything you don't do?" I ask, because he's an animal and the phrase doesn't fit him.

He laughs and shakes his head. "I'm game for everything and anything."

"You're also a dumbass," I tell him, and it's his turn to give me the middle finger before he stalks out.

I glance at the clock, and it's a quarter to seven. I have only a few minutes to straighten up the mess Liam made and the few half-filled coffee cups that have sat out so long they have mold growing on top of the liquid.

I make quick work of the small things, opting to throw out the used mugs. We should really use paper, especially since we get called away a lot to help stranded drivers. Ceramic mugs don't fit in the truck's cupholder, and I'm not one to reheat my coffee when I get back to the garage after.

"Hello!" Lulu's voice echoes through the garage, and my heart leaps inside my chest.

I take a quick glance around the bays and our office area, and things are the best they're going to get. I can't sugarcoat it. It's a working garage filled with grease, dirt, and tools everywhere.

"Back here," I say, heading toward her voice. She must've come through the front that's only used by customers.

As I round the corner, she walks through the garage entrance, and we nearly collide.

"Hey," I say, suddenly nervous, which isn't like me.

We haven't seen each other since the day we met, but we've been texting here and there, though nothing too much.

"This is super cute." Her gaze roams around the

garage, not stopping for much longer than a second on certain areas. "This is a dream job for me."

I can't stop my entire forehead from pinching down. "Are you feeling okay?" There's no way a dirty place like this could be called a dream job by anyone, especially her.

"I'm fine, but this—" she waves her hand around "—is an organizer's paradise. The challenge of it all."

"You're an odd bird, Lulu."

"Normal is so boring, Oliver," she says with a playful smirk. "Can I look around?"

"Yeah." I motion toward the area behind me. "Look wherever you want. I'll just sit at my desk and observe."

She sets her bag down on an empty chair near the office area. "How long have you been here?"

"We bought the business ten years ago from my stepdad's buddy."

"Impressive. What were you? Eighteen?"

I let out a bark of laughter. "I wish. I was twenty-five and just out of the military. I had saved up some cash while I was in there and figured, why not own my own business."

"Wait." She spins around, staring straight at me as her eyes roam over my face. "That would make you…"

"Thirty-five."

"Damn," she whispers, and that one word is like a dagger to my heart.

"I know I'm old."

She reaches out, placing her hand on my arm. "No, not old. You're aging like a fine wine, Oliver. I wouldn't have pegged you for a day over twenty-eight."

"And you are?"

"Twenty-four," she replies.

"You're so young," I whisper. "Too young."

"Too young for what?" she asks, taking a step closer and staring up at me with those big brown doe eyes.

"Well...I..." I've never been one to fumble around, but this woman has me off-kilter. She's too sweet. Too innocent-looking to be around a meathead like me.

But with the way she's looking at me and the crackle in the air, I can't help myself. Young though she may be, my entire body is craving to touch her, to taste her. I reach out, snake my arm around her waist, and pull her flush against me.

"For this," I whisper, bending my neck to bring our mouths closer together.

Her breath hitches, and her eyes somehow get bigger.

"Unless you don't..." I start to say because maybe I've been reading the chemistry all wrong. But before I can finish the statement, Lulu pops up on her tiptoes and presses her lips to mine.

The soft contact is all I need to unleash the desire

I've felt since the moment we met. That day when I tackled her, lying on top of her, staring down into her frightened eyes, something shifted in me. Something I'd never felt before in my life. I chalked it up to the adrenaline of the moment, but no matter what I did, I couldn't shake it.

"Oliver," she moans against my lips, making me kiss her deeper and harder.

The moment is like something out of a cheesy romance movie where the world falls away except the two of us. Nothing else exists. Nothing else matters.

"Well, now." Liam's voice cuts through the air.

I groan in frustration as Lulu starts to pull away. I open my eyes, finding her big brown ones staring back at me.

"Who do we have here?" he asks as he walks in our direction. He's still a cockblock as an adult, which is more annoying than when he was one as a kid.

"Don't you have somewhere to be?" I ask, my voice filled with frustration.

"Forgot my wallet," he says as I track his movement with my gaze. "And you are?" His eyes linger a little too long on Lulu not to rub me the wrong way.

"Lulu."

"She's a friend," I interrupt her response because my brother will pitch a fit about having anything moved out of its current place.

Her eyebrows rise as he says, "Looks like a little more than friends."

"Isn't Sharla waiting for you?"

He snags his wallet off his desk and shoves it in his back pocket, his gaze wandering down the length of her body. "Sharla's not going anywhere, Oli, relax. It's nice to finally put a face with the name."

I growl, wanting to tell him to fuck off and leave, but I know that'll only make him stay longer. He's annoying like that. "Can you go now?"

"Sure," he says with a smile, "we'll talk more about this later."

"After Vegas," I reply.

He nods and finally walks toward the exit. "See you soon, brother. And, Lulu, it was a pleasure."

"Bye," I bite out, done with him.

When he's gone, I do my best to smooth over the awkwardness caused by his interruption. "I'm sorry."

"For what?" she asks.

"He's a jerk."

"He didn't seem that bad."

"He was on his best behavior. Trust me when I tell you to steer clear of him. He's nothing but trouble."

"Brothers...am I right?"

"Do you have one?"

She shakes her head. "A sister and she isn't any better."

"Do you wanna grab something to eat after this?" I ask, shooting my shot because I have been dying to ask her out but didn't feel the vibes were there on her part until the kiss.

Her smile is immediate, and I know I have her. "I'd love that. I just want to take a few minutes to look everything over to make a list of supplies I'll need, and then we can go."

"Perfect."

She doesn't waste any time moving away from me, heading straight toward the bank of cabinets. They are filled with so many parts, both big and small, that I'm not sure she'll want to continue any further once she gets a good look. The size of the job has to be daunting. It's why I gave up on organizing everything years ago. This isn't just our mess, but that of the guy who owned this before us too.

"Wow," she says as her fingers skate over a shelf of tiny boxes filled with bolts of every size. "There's a lot here."

"Too much." I drop down into the chair at my desk and keep my eyes on her as she continues down the row of cabinets. "Sorry."

"This is great," she says, confusing me. Nothing about the contents of the cabinets is great. They're a freaking mess, and every time I open a door, I'm quick to close it. "This is going to be fun, actually."

I'm so shocked by her words, I could practically fall out of my chair. "Fun? What's fun about that?"

"Do you think a really hard-to-fix car is fun?"

"It's a challenge."

"That's this for me. Organizing a laundry room is easy. But this—" she waves her hands around the dingy garage "—is the best kind of challenge."

I'm not going to argue with her. If this is a challenge, then that means it will take a lot of time. If she needs a lot of time to finish the job, that means she'll be here a lot. That is a win-win for me, and I'm not going to do anything to talk her out of it.

"Do you have a date you need this done by?" she asks as she glances at me from across the garage.

"No. Take as long as you need. It's been like this for years."

"It might take me a few months since I'll be fitting in this job when I have time."

Months would be perfect. Any amount of time would be great as long as it means she'll be here. I'll handle Liam. Lulu is too good for him, and I know he is falling for Sharla even if he pretends it is nothing more than fun. "That's fine."

Her smile widens. "Then I'm done. We can go eat."

"You're done?" I can't keep the shock out of my voice. "Really?"

She starts to move back toward my desk, carefully stepping around shit Liam left out on the floor. "Yeah. I'll need a lot of things. Too much to make one list for right now."

"I'll pay for them."

"This is a gift."

"Your time is a gift, Lulu. The supplies, I'll buy."

She opens her mouth to argue, but I can't let her go out of pocket to fix our disaster of a garage.

"No arguments."

She gives me a tight smile, and I don't know her well enough to figure out if she's annoyed or happy. "Fine, but I get to pick the restaurant tonight."

"Burgers?" I ask.

She shakes her head as she sits down at Liam's desk, looking completely out of place here. "Pizza."

"You're my kind of girl," I say without thinking.

Her cheeks turn the prettiest shade of pink. "I like my food, even if my hips don't."

"What's wrong with your hips?" I've checked them out more than once, and when I say they're perfect, I mean they're perfect. My hands would have a field day on them if I ever have the chance to get her naked.

"They're biggish. Thick."

"No one wants a bone," I tell her, my mouth already salivating at the thought of touching them. "I want something to hold. The thicker, the better."

"Really?" She blinks a few times like I'm lying and she doesn't believe me.

"Do you like a bony guy?"

"Well, no. I need something to snuggle."

"Exactly." I smirk, wanting to wrap her in my arms immediately, but then I remember we're in the garage and she isn't my girl.

"Then pizza it is, with extra cheese."

"Attagirl. You got a spot in mind?"

"Vito and Nick's?"

"The best. But I can polish off an entire pizza myself, so we'd better get two."

"I like your style, Oliver."

I stand and give her a big smile. "I'll drive."

"Great because my rental sucks."

My eyebrows rise. "You're still in a rental? What happened with Randall?"

"I'm meeting him tomorrow to buy a new one."

I make a mental note to call Randall tomorrow morning and make sure he gives her the best deal possible. I want this woman around, and that doesn't start by my stepdad ripping her off to make a few extra bucks.

I motion for her to head toward the exit as I turn off the lights, ready to lock up and run out of here. "Do you need help?"

She glances over her shoulder at me. "You want to come?"

I nod. "If you want me there, I'll be there."

"I'll think about it over pizza," she says as we step outside.

I turn to lock up the door, and I smile. That wasn't a no. No one wants to waste a day at a car dealership, but I'll do just about anything to spend time with this woman, including suffering the torture of buying a car I'm not even going to drive. "Pepperoni?" I ask as

I slide my key into the lock, ready to get out of this place.

"Duh. Is there any other topping?"

When I turn back toward her, she's staring at my ass.

I have her.

CHAPTER 5
LULU

"I'M SORRY," I say to Oliver as we sit at his stepfather's desk, waiting for him to finish up in the finance office.

"For what?"

I shrug and leave my shoulders slumped forward. "I'm sure you have better things to do today than this."

"Nope. There's nowhere I'd rather be."

I blink a few times, staring at him. No one likes going to a car dealership. Stepfather or not, this isn't on anyone's things-I-love-to-do list. "You're a good liar."

Tiny lines form near the corners of his eyes as he laughs. "I'm not lying."

"Yeah, you are. No one wants to spend their day off here."

"If I didn't want to come, I wouldn't be here. It's that simple, Lulu."

"Are you here because you love car dealerships, or are you here because…" My voice trails off because I don't want to say it.

Last night was great. The conversation flowed so easily between us. The man wasn't lying because I watched him polish off an entire thin-crust pizza with extra cheese and extra pepperoni like it was nothing at all. I made it through a quarter of the other pizza before I felt like I'd need to be rolled out of there.

I don't remember the last time it was so easy to be around someone who was still a stranger. And don't even get me started on the kiss before his brother walked in. It made my toes curl in my shoes. I thought he'd try to kiss me again after we had pizza, but it didn't happen, and to say I was disappointed would be an understatement.

Maybe he changed his mind after our tongues did the tango. Maybe he realized I wasn't a good kisser and the entire thing turned him off. Now he's here out of a sense of obligation to help me since my car was destroyed and he feels sorry for me.

"Because?" he asks with a raised eyebrow.

"I don't know," I whisper, unable to make myself say the words I want him to hear. I can usually handle rejection, but there is something about him at this point in my life that would make the sting hurt more than usual.

He reaches across the small space between us and places his hand on top of mine. "I'm here for you."

I peer up at him as my belly flutters. His palm is warm against my skin, and when his fingers curl ever so slightly around mine, my heart rate picks up. "For me?"

God, I sound so lame. Anyone with a brain would know that. He isn't here for a visit with the old man.

"Why is that surprising?"

"Well, I don't know."

"Because I didn't kiss you again last night?" he asks, shocking me.

My eyes widen for a brief moment. "Kind of."

"Did you want me to kiss you again?"

I'm speechless for a second. He's so direct. More direct than anyone else I've ever known besides the people in my family. "Yes," I say breathlessly.

"Were you sad I didn't?"

"Yes," I whisper.

"It won't happen again."

My stomach drops as the realization he doesn't feel the same crashes over me. "Oh. I understand." I try to pull my hand away, but he tightens his grip.

"No, you don't. You misunderstand me, Lulu. I won't let you leave me again without giving you a kiss. Last night, when we got back to the garage, you ran away like your ass was on fire. Figured you didn't want to kiss me, but now I know, and I won't make that mistake again."

My belly flutters again. I did run away like my ass was on fire because it literally was about to be. I overdid it on the pizza and the cheese. My stomach was having none of it, and I had to rush home before I had an accident in front of the most beautiful man I'd ever met.

"Sorry about that," Randall, Oliver's stepdad, says as he walks up to the desk, killing the moment.

Twice now, his family has ruined things, and I almost feel at home with their streak because it's the kind of shit my family would do too.

"Did anything catch your eye on the way in?" Randall asks as he sits down in his chair across from us.

"Straight to business, huh?" Oliver says, his hand not moving from mine as I swing my gaze to him.

"Figured you wanted out of here quick," Randall replies without being the least bit rattled.

Oliver grunts.

For a split second, I think we're going to be out of here before I have a chance to get a car.

"Sorry if I was being rude. It's nice to meet you, Lulu. Oliver said you need a new car. Did anything strike you on the way in?"

I shift in my seat, uncomfortable with the entire exchange. "It did."

"Excellent. Which one?"

"The black SUV right outside the door."

"Ah. Good choice. Do you want to test drive it?"

I nod. "It may be out of my price range, though. I'd hate to waste your time."

"Ignore the sticker. I can work up a quote while Oliver takes you out there to look on the inside. I'll grab the key. Good?"

"Perfect," Oliver answers.

"Good," Randall says before he pushes himself up from the seat and stalks away.

"Why were you mean to him?" I ask Oliver.

"I wasn't. Randall isn't the nicest, but he could at least say hello. We're not strangers. He's my stepdad, for shit's sake. A simple greeting would be nice."

"Well, it's his work."

"If you walk into the bar, does your dad say hello or just ask what you want to order?"

He had a point. "He'd say hello."

"Exactly. Everything with Randall is business. I deal with him because he makes buying a new vehicle easy, but it would be nice if he could act like a normal human being since he practically raised me."

"That sucks."

"Yeah," Oliver mutters. "He's always been an asshole and I've come to ignore it, but he doesn't know you and could at least act civilized."

"I don't mind."

"You should."

"I don't, though. I just want the SUV and to dip as quickly as possible."

"Then he's your man."

"Keys," Randall says, shaking them near my side. "You two go look at the inside or take it for a test drive, and I'll work up that price."

I take the keys from his hand. "Thanks."

"No problem," he says before walking away.

"Come on," I say to Oliver, squeezing his hands that are still intertwined with mine on the arm of my chair. "I'm dying to see in the inside and try that baby out. If he gives me a good price and I like the SUV, we'll be out of here before we're forced to make small talk with him."

"You have a point."

"You know I'm right," I say to him. "Up you go, big man."

He chuckles as he stands and follows me toward the glass front doors of the dealership.

"I think the SUV is going to be perfect for my business."

"It has a good engine on it, but you're going to pay a ton for gas with that hemi."

"Oh. I didn't notice," I say, playing stupid, but I totally did. "Is that good?" I know the thing is going to purr when I start it. Hemi engines always do.

"If you like horsepower and speed, it is."

"I want something that when a car hits it, they bounce off and not the other way around."

"That'll be this one," he says as we stop in front of the beautiful black SUV.

Everything is black. The grill. The wheels. The

rims. Even the windows are tinted. "I love it so much," I say as I drag my finger over the newly polished paint. "I need to drive it." I push the button on the remote, and the doors unlock, sending a thrill through me.

"Do you know what to do with this much power?"

"Handle it like a boss," I tell him as I open the door and climb inside.

Oliver's laugh makes me giggle in return. "You're something else, Lulu. You're funny as shit."

"You won't be laughing when I handle the turns."

"That's hard to do when the speed limit is twenty-five in the city."

"Can we take it on the freeway?"

His happy face falls instantly. "You want to take this on the freeway?"

I nod quickly. "Well, of course."

"Then let's do it. I want to see what you think is fast."

I raise an eyebrow, loving a challenge. "If there's no traffic, I'm going to make your heart stop."

"You already do," he whispers.

"What?" I ask, because I'm not sure I heard him right.

"I'm ready," he says, but I know that's not what he muttered before.

"Buckle up, buddy," I tell him as I reach behind my shoulder and grab the seat belt. "This is going to be a wild ride."

"Oh boy," he mutters as he grabs the seat belt and clicks in before gripping the handle on the side door.

"Scared?" I ask, teasing him. I'm going to drive like a grandma. I already have enough tickets, and the last thing I need is more. But it was fun to joke about it and see the panic start to rise behind his eyes.

"A little." He gives me a nervous smile as I ease the car into drive.

"It's good to get your blood pumping a little each day."

"I'd prefer it not to be from fear of dying."

I chuckle. "You're too easy," I tell him, finally coming clean. "I'm not going to hurt this baby before I have a chance to buy her. Anyway, I have too many tickets right now to risk getting another one. They're so damn expensive too."

He lets out a long breath and touches his chest. "Thank God. I didn't really want to meet my maker today."

"Even if I were going to haul ass, what makes you think I would be bad at it?"

He's quiet for a moment as I pull onto the busy street. Chicago traffic is a nightmare. It doesn't matter what time of day or where you are in the city, it's always crowded.

"If you say it's because I'm a woman, I'm going to—"

"No," he snaps. "It's not that. I'm not an asshole."

I tighten my hold on the steering wheel, loving the

way the SUV handles. The tires grip the road, and the heaviness makes me feel like I'm driving a tank. "Then why?"

"Because I don't trust anyone else's driving except my own," he says.

I glance over at him, seeing his hand now on his knee, and his knuckles are white. "I'm an expert driver."

"Sure," he mumbles and points out the windshield. "The road."

I sigh and swing my gaze back to the road in front of us, which I knew was empty since everyone hustled through the light just ahead of us before it could turn red. "I love this uneasy side of you."

"Sadist."

"Maybe," I say with a smirk on my lips. "But you seem so in control and comfortable all the time. It's nice to see there's another side of you."

"It's hard to be in control when it's not my hands on the wheel."

I ignore his statement and focus on the car. "How does she sound to you?"

"She?"

"The SUV."

"Oh." He rubs his hand up and down his leg before it stops on his knee again, holding on for dear life. "It sounds great."

"And she feels right?"

"She feels perfect."

"I think so too. I'm buying her as long as Randall doesn't pull some crazy numbers out of nowhere."

"The deal will be good."

"I hope so. I don't want to fall in love with this thing and then have it ripped away from me a few minutes later. I'd be heartbroken."

"I won't let it happen. Randall knows the deal."

I glance his direction and give him a small smile. "I don't know how I'm ever going to thank you for everything."

"You've done enough."

"Not really."

"The garage is a huge job."

"It is." And although I don't mind how much work it is going to be, I'm really doing it so that I can spend more time with him.

I like Oliver. I like everything about him except for his inability to be relaxed in a car with me as the driver. I can see myself with a man like him, and not a single red flag has popped up either.

"Well, let's head back."

"Oh, thank God," he breathes.

"Seriously?" I ask, but I'm teasing him, and I think he's teasing me. "I drove like a ninety-year-old woman."

"I know, and it was scary as fuck."

"You're so dramatic. Who hurt you?"

"My mom. She hit a house with me in the back seat when I was little. I never got over it."

I snapped my head to the right. "What?"

"No lie. She hit a literal brick house. Smashed right through a tree on the way too. Never been so fuckin' scared in my entire life."

Now I understand where his fear of not having his own hands on the steering wheel comes from.

"And then, as a tow truck driver, I see every horrible wreck imaginable."

"Maybe not the right career path."

He lets out a nervous laugh. "Nah. I like helping people when they need it."

"Like me."

"Like you."

"Am I the first woman you tackled out of the way of a speeding car?"

"Yeah, Lulu. You're the first."

"Well, lucky me," I tell him. "If it were anyone else in your place, they might have let me become roadkill." I pull into the parking spot on the lot where the car had been earlier. Oliver's entire body immediately relaxes as if someone took a little air out of him. "We made it. No houses were injured in the test drive either."

He shakes his head as he reaches for the handle, looking like he needs to jump out as quickly as possible. "Good job," he says as soon as his feet are firmly planted on the cement. "I had all the faith in the world in you."

"Uh-huh," I mutter as I climb out, nearly having

to jump down because the SUV is so high. "I love this damn thing."

"Then let's go find Randall and get the hell out of here."

I chuckle as I follow him inside, liking this uncool side of a man who always seems so together. I did that to him, and I kind of like it.

CHAPTER 6
OLIVER

THIRTY MINUTES AGO, Lulu messaged me that there was an issue at her place, asking me if I could come over and fix it.

Now, I'm standing outside her front door, staring at the ornate door knocker that must've cost an arm and a leg. It is totally Lulu's style. A little over the top and beautiful.

I knock twice, looking from side to side at the empty neighborhood. It is late, but not late enough that the area should be as deserted as it is. My fingers tighten around the bag of tools I brought in case she doesn't have her own.

The door opens, and Lulu gives me the biggest smile while tipping up on her toes. She looks way too happy for a woman who's having a problem. "Hey," she says in her sugary-sweet voice that makes my blood pump a little harder. "Thanks for coming."

"Hey. Anytime. What's up?" I shiver as a gust of winter wind whips around me.

She pulls the door open wider and motions for me to come inside. I take a large stride, making sure to keep my dirty boots on the rug near the doorway. Her floors are dark wood and glisten from being newly polished, or maybe they're always this clean. I wouldn't doubt it when it comes to her.

"I came home from meeting with my last client today, and the dishwasher won't turn on."

Not an emergency, but I still would've shown up even if she'd told me what the issue was before I agreed to come. The woman could ask me to do anything, and I'd do it without asking any questions.

"You're in luck," I tell her as I toe off my boots, careful not to get the melting snow, dirt, and garage oil everywhere. "Dishwashers are easy."

She chuckles as she holds out her hands, waiting for me to remove my jacket. "You haven't met one as old as mine."

"It's deserted outside," I say, making small talk.

"A winter storm is coming."

"Damn," I mutter. I haven't turned on the news in a few days, and I haven't received any alerts on my phone. George and Kramer are on shift at the garage, so at least any issues that come up for motorists in the storm overnight will be covered.

"I'm over it."

"Me too." I long for the dog days of summer

when the sun scorches your flesh and the only calls I get are for wrecks and flat tires. Winter causes an entirely different set of issues for drivers, and none of them are usually easy. Never mind freezing my ass off as I hook them up to the truck.

"It's back here," she says, walking in front of me down a long hall toward the back of her house.

As I walk, I soak in the decorations and colors. Everything is dark, almost like she's allergic to color. I thought her place would be filled with bright colors, but boy, was I wrong.

"You like the color black?" I ask as I tilt my head up, noticing that even the ceiling is painted dark.

"I go for the moody vibe."

"Moody," I grumble, but if I'm being honest, I like it. Her style is a contrast to the stark-white walls of my place that the previous owners had painted. I don't have the time or vision to change them, but this...this is beautiful.

"Do you like it?"

"I do," I tell her as we enter the kitchen, the one room I'd assume would be the opposite of the others I've seen.

But the kitchen is like something out of a magazine. The cabinets are matte black and somehow feel warm with the stained butcher block countertops. The walls are the same color as the cabinets but with a slight sheen. The place is absolutely stunning and something straight out of a designer magazine.

"Wow."

Lulu glances at me with the biggest smile on her face. "It's my favorite room in the house."

"I can see why."

"I'm glad you like it."

Like doesn't even begin to describe how I feel about the space. It is magnificent. I could cook in here every day of the week and never get sick of looking at it.

"Here's the old beast," she says from the other side of the massive island, pointing downward. "She's finicky."

"That happens sometimes when you get old."

When my gaze drops to the dishwasher, I stare at it in surprise. It's not old. It's been here maybe five years, tops.

"This is new," I tell her as I set my bag of tools down next to it.

"It's not new."

"Sweetheart, I have appliances older than you at my place." I kneel down, hating the way my knees ache as they hit the hardwood.

"That doesn't surprise me."

"What's it doing?" I open the door, finding the bottom filled with water.

"I turn it on, and it shuts off. Just dies and beeps at me a few times."

"Mine doesn't beep."

"The app on my phone isn't giving me an error."

"Your dishwasher has an app?"

She nods. "Don't they all?"

I grunt and shake my head. "No. They don't all have apps. We didn't have apps back in the day."

She touches her chest and gasps. "How did you do things?" she teases and smacks my shoulders. "I'm not that young that I don't remember those days, Oli. But whoever had the house before me made sure every appliance had an app to make things easier. Technology can do that for people."

"Does it really?" I ask her, peering up at her pretty face as I kneel on the floor, wishing I were in this position for another reason and not just to fix her dishwasher.

"I got us some takeout from the bar. You hungry?"

"I could eat," I tell her as I pull out the empty dishrack and set it to the side. But in reality, I am starving. I didn't have time to grab something to eat before I came over here. I didn't want to keep her waiting and figured I'd stop on the way back home.

"I'll heat everything up while you do your thing."

"You got a deal," I tell her, already knowing what the issue is. It's a simple fix. Something she could've done without any real mechanical skill. And I'm sure this isn't the first time she's had this problem with the machine, but I'm not about to split hairs and call her out for it.

I need to make it clear to her that she doesn't need to come up with a reason to get me to come over. I'll come for any reason because I want to spend time with her, even if that means painting another one of her ceilings black, and I hate doing that shit.

"I had my cousin give me everything to make Italian beef sandwiches. Is that okay?"

Is it okay? The girl totally speaks my language when it comes to food. First, we had killer burgers, then the best damn pizza in the world, and now we're having Italian beef? "Perfect."

"Excellent," she says, sounding a little like Bill and Ted from their excellent adventure because the girl is so blissfully happy even when shit is going wrong.

"You got a bowl and something to scoop out this water?"

"Sure. One sec."

I watch her over the island as she moves around the kitchen like she's floating across the floor. Within a few seconds, she has a bowl and a few options for me to remove the water from the bottom of her fancy-ass dishwasher.

"This good?"

I peer up at her, meeting her gaze. "Perfect," I whisper, but I could be talking more about her than the actual shit she brought me.

The sound of pebbles pinging against glass draws our attention toward the bank of windows near her table. "Is that…"

"Ice," she says. "The storm's started."

"Shit," I mumble, knowing it's going to be a bitch

to get home if the roads are icy. My truck is great in the snow, but the tires turn into skates when there isn't any traction. "I should've known when I passed a few salt trucks out there, but it didn't register."

Nothing registered on my drive over. I was too busy trying to follow the GPS to her place and too damn excited about seeing her to notice much of anything. The world could've been on fire all around me, and I wouldn't have seen the flames. I was laser-focused on my goal, which was to get here and spend time with Lulu, even if that meant fixing her shit.

"Ice is the worst," she says as she moves back around the island, leaving me to work.

"No car in the world can handle it, but everyone sure as hell tries." I pick up the biggest measuring cup, using it to fish out as much water as I can before having to go down a size.

"You'd know, wouldn't you?"

"Yep. I hate it more than snow." I am thankful I have the night off, and it's now George and Kramer's issue. I am fairly certain they are cursing me for it too. They won't be spending the night playing video games like they do most graveyard shifts when things are calm.

"If it gets too bad, you can stay here."

My arm freezes in midair as my stomach flips over. "You'd be okay with that?"

"Of course. Can't have my hero driving home on dangerous roads."

"Huh," I whisper, suddenly feeling like this was all planned.

A dishwasher like this probably gets a blocked filter at least once a year. This isn't the first time it's been fixed, based on the length of time she has to have been living in this place—and if I'm going off the decorations, it's been more than a handful of years. She knew the weather forecast and isn't at all surprised by the ice storm that's brewing outside like I am. And then the invitation to stay over came way too easy.

She wants me here for more than her dishwasher.

"How's it going?" she asks, coming around the corner of the island with napkins and silverware. "Is it bad?" She places the items on the table, carefully arranging them.

"No. It should only take a few minutes." I scoop more water, dumping it into the bowl she gave me. It's tedious work, but I've had to do things far worse than spend time with a pretty woman.

"Really? Food's almost ready anyway, so it's perfect timing."

A little too perfect, but I'm not going to complain or call her out about anything. Having a great meal and talking with her is no hardship. There isn't anything, even an impending storm, that could've stopped me from coming over here tonight.

Once enough of the water is removed, I make quick work of the filter, cleaning it off completely.

Lulu is competent enough to do this herself, and I'd bet my truck she's done it herself before. She had the meal perfectly timed to the number of minutes it would take me to complete this.

"All done," I tell her as I twist the filter back in.

"Wow. You're fast. Must've been an easy fix, huh?"

I laugh softly, knowing her game as I slide the rack back into place and close the door. "Yeah. Easy."

"You want chips with your sandwich? I have salt and vinegar or sour cream."

"A girl after my own heart."

"You want both?"

"Vinegar," I tell her as she stands in front of two unopened bags on the countertop.

"Good choice," she says as she grabs the blue bag and heads toward the table, while I push myself upward, ignoring the cracking noise coming from my knees. "Let me wash up."

"I left a towel for you by the sink."

Of course she did. The woman thinks of everything. "Did you design everything yourself?" I ask as I pump the soap dispenser twice, instantly hit by the scent of vanilla.

"Yeah. My mom helped a bit, but she's more about light colors and florals."

"Complete opposites."

Lulu laughs as she assembles the sandwiches. "She can appreciate my vision, even if it isn't her own."

"That's sweet." I haven't met a person in her family who isn't nice, just like she is. They are so very unlike my people, and it isn't lost on me how my family is probably more abnormal than hers is.

"My mom is the best."

"The tile is something." I stare at the matte black tiles all perfectly arranged on the wall behind the sink and underneath the cabinets. Each one is unique and handmade and had to cost a damn near fortune for a kitchen this size.

"My cousin Tate and I made each one at a local ceramic place that our friend owns. It took us months to make them all."

"Damn," I whisper, completely impressed. By the looks of her, I'd have assumed she'd bought them at a fancy tile store. Never in a million years did I think she made each one of them by hand.

"Come. Sit," she says, holding two plates with some of the largest Italian beef sandwiches I've ever seen. "They're not as good when they're cold."

"I'd eat that any way you'd give it to me."

She sucks in a breath, staring at me like she is about to pounce, which is odd. I was talking about the sandwich, but the look in her eyes makes me think she was hoping I was talking about something else. "I'm sure you would."

As soon as she sets the plates down on the table, I grab her wrist, stopping her from sitting. She peers over her shoulder at me, our eyes locking. "Sweetheart, tell me something."

"What?" she asks, and her voice is husky and rough.

"Did you really need me to fix your dishwasher, or did you call me over here for something else?"

She swallows hard as her eyes widen. "Like what?"

I caress the pulse point on her wrist with my thumb. "We never got to finish what we started at the garage."

"I didn't think you'd want…"

That's all she needed to say. I know what she wants but can't bring herself to ask for. She is probably worried I'll reject her, which is bananas because the woman is mint and way too classy for a dipshit like me.

I yank her toward me, our bodies colliding. "You want me?" I stare down at her as her lips part, and her tongue pokes out like it's beckoning me.

"Yes," she breathes as her gaze drops to my lips. "But if you don't want to, I—"

"I've never wanted anything more," I say before pressing my mouth to hers in a clash of lips and teeth, ravenous for her more than any sandwich.

She moans as I snake my hand around her back, my fingers finding her neck, wanting to control everything. Her moan grows louder as my hold tightens and my kiss deepens.

If my hand hadn't been holding her, she would be on the floor because her body goes limp as she gives me her entire body weight.

"I want you so bad," she murmurs against my lips.

That's all any man needs to hear to lose absolute control. Fuck the Italian beef. I have something better than that in my mouth. I have an Italian princess, and if I am a lucky man, I'll know how every inch of her body tastes after tonight.

I pull back, staring down at her eyes, which are now soft and hazy. "What do you want, Lulu?"

"Everything," she whispers. "It's been too long, and my body is dying for yours. I need you."

My restraint slips, what little of it I had left anyway. I lift Lulu, placing her ass on the countertop without breaking our kiss.

My fingers move to the hem of her T-shirt before lifting it up, hating that the shirt isn't button-down. Our mouths only separate for the briefest of moments as I yank the T-shirt over her head, disposing of it somewhere nearby. Her skin is hot underneath my palms, and I groan at the softness against my calluses.

I drag my hands to her breasts, feeling the coarseness of her lace bra and the weight of her in my palms. I'm in heaven. And if this isn't what the afterlife is like, I don't want it. I have a beautiful, half-naked woman in front of me who's begging for me to touch her, take her, make her mine. Absolute paradise.

As she wraps her legs around my waist, I realize my mistake. There's no way to get her pants off in this position. *Way to go, Oli.*

Without saying a word, I lift Lulu from the counter, setting her feet flat on the floor. She doesn't protest or ask any questions. Her mouth's too busy with mine to say anything. My fingers work at the button and zipper of her jeans before I yank them down and reach for her underwear. But to my shock, I find nothing but bare skin.

I can feel her smile against my lips as my movement halts for a split second when I realize there's nothing between us now. She kicks her jeans to the side, standing in front of me in nothing more than her bra.

My hands move to her back, unclasping the little hooks that were created to torture men and make having sex more difficult than it needs to be. They are nothing more than a modern-day chastity belt for the top half.

I break the kiss, the hunger inside me so deep, I can't hold back anymore. "Up you go," I tell her as I push her upward back onto the countertop before falling to my knees. "I need to taste you."

She spreads her legs wide without my having to tell her. She wants this as much as I do. I glance up, still in disbelief that this is my life. She looks down at me with a smirk, moving her left leg from side to side.

"I'm waiting," she says in a sultry voice.

"Fuck," I growl and loop my arms underneath her legs, spreading her wide.

She gasps, shocked by my speed, but that doesn't stop me. I lean forward and dive into her pussy like I'm a starved man and she's the meal.

There's a loud thump from above, but I don't stop to see what it is. I'm too busy tasting her sweetness and loving the way her fingers tangle in my hair. She gasps for air as I suck at her clit and kiss her everywhere, being messy because I want it all... I want her.

She tries to close her legs, but I hold them firm, not letting her get away from the orgasm I hope is building inside her.

"Fuck, I'm going to..."

"Come for me, baby," I say against her skin before going in harder this time, driving her over the cliff.

"Oliver," she moans before she screams out her pleasure, her fingers twisting my hair to the point of pain, but I don't care. She could rip out every last strand as long as I can hear her moan my name like this again.

When her body finally goes limp and she's gasping for air, I know I did what needed to be done. Lulu Gallo is mine.

CHAPTER 7
LULU

I STARTLE AWAKE, my heart pounding uncontrollably in my bed as I sit up. Was I having a bad dream? No. Not that I remember, but something has me bolting upright out of the deepest sleep I've had in weeks.

Suddenly, a pounding on my front door has me sucking in a breath of air like I'm a goldfish out of water.

"Lulu, open the damn door!" my sister screams so loud, she has to be waking up the entire neighborhood.

"What the hell," Oliver says at my side as he rubs his eyes, his sleep shot to shit by Zoey too.

"It's my sister. Something has to be wrong." I jump out of bed, finding something to wear. I grab whatever's closest and yank it on, needing to get to

Zoey as quickly as possible. "Go back to sleep. I've got her."

My body trembles as I stalk down the hallway toward the front door, leaving Oliver in my bedroom.

"Coming!" I yell out, hoping she'll stop making so much noise. I undo the locks and finally open the door.

Zoey is standing outside, mascara running down her face, eyes red and puffy, and her hair a mess.

I gasp as my eyes widen. "Oh my God. Get in here," I tell her as the snow and ice rain down from the sky at a maddening pace from the storm.

She doesn't move. She trembles as more tears start to stream down her face in a fresh wave. I reach out, grabbing her arms before I haul her into the foyer, wanting to get her warm and figure out what the hell has her so upset.

"What's wrong, Zo?" I scan her body, looking for injuries, but it's hard to see anything with her knee-length winter coat.

"He…" She wipes at her cheek with the back of her hand. "They…"

I bend down, helping her remove her fur-lined boots. Whatever she needs to tell me isn't going to take place in the foyer. She needs to sit, and I have to find out everything that happened because Zoey doesn't get upset with much, and she's absolutely beside herself tonight. I don't think I've ever seen her like this in my entire life.

"Come on, sissy. Let's get you warm," I tell her, guiding her to the living room couch, not bothering to take her coat from her. "I need you to tell me what happened."

Her bottom isn't on the couch for three seconds when she blurts out, "Mark."

My blood goes cold. Mark is a fuckwad she's been seeing casually the last few months. They fool around and go to dinner, but neither of them has made any commitments to each other. My sister is fine with that. She doesn't want to be tied down and thinks Mark is only a good-time kind of guy anyway.

But I've never liked him. When I look at him, I never see an ounce of kindness. He oozes self-absorbed asshole. And no matter how many times I've told Zoey that he gives me the icks, she hasn't seen him the same way and has always reassured me that he was a decent enough guy.

"What did Mark do?" I do my best to keep my voice calm, but my insides are burning up. I already have visions of murder and mayhem, and all of them involve me putting an end to Mark if he hurt my sister. "Did he hit you?"

She shakes her head as her bottom lip trembles.

Reaching out, I take her hands in mine, rubbing my thumb across the delicate skin on the top. "Baby, what has you so worked up?"

The silence between us as I wait for her to answer seems to stretch on for an eternity.

"Tell me, Zo," I beg as the panic inside me intensifies.

She drops her gaze as she opens her mouth and starts to speak, "We were fooling around, you know, and things were good. We had some wine…a lot of wine, actually."

"Okay," I say when she stops. "What else?"

"Mark likes to be adventurous in the bedroom."

I pull in my lips, clamping them together so I don't start losing my shit on her. She's not the one who needs to hear the words. They're all meant for Mark because I know the next words out of her mouth are going to send me into a spiral.

"Tonight, he tied me up and blindfolded me. I was okay with it, for the most part. Not completely, but I never had any reason to say no to him."

The hairs on the back of my neck stand, and with every sentence, my fear only gets worse.

"Once I got over the initial panic of not being able to move or see, things seemed to be going well."

I don't ever want to think sex with another person seems to be "going well." No one should be uncomfortable to the point where they're panicked unless that is the emotion they are going for.

"He told me the panic would heighten the sensations and that I should just lie there and feel. He said it was all about my pleasure tonight."

I am a razor's edge from losing my shit, but I somehow stop myself from reacting. Zoey doesn't need to hear my criticism, even if it is pointed at Mark and not her.

Zoey sniffles, and the sound breaks my heart. My sister and I are thick as thieves. There isn't a secret I have that she doesn't know. We are each other's best friends, and it has been that way since the day she was born.

"It was enjoyable at first, but it was hard for me to orgasm with my arms and legs tied to the corners of the bed. I'd never felt so naked in my entire life."

My mind snags on the fact that she was splayed out, unable to move. All four limbs were secured to the bed. What an awful position to be in with someone you don't completely trust.

"I can't imagine, Zo."

"You don't want to," she says with a soft voice that quavers. "Things were going okay until…"

I swallow down the bile that's rising in my throat, getting higher with each word. I've never felt more murderous in my entire life than I do in this moment.

"Mark's mouth was on me. He said he was going to force me to orgasm, but then I realized there were more than two hands on my body. I thought it was his hands on my breasts because every sensation was so overwhelming. But I felt his hand on my hip, and I knew there was more than just him in the bed with me."

When people say they see red, they sure as hell

mean it. The amount of anger that burns inside me has flames of destruction flickering in my eyes.

"I'm going to fucking kill him."

Zoey squeezes my hands. "I flipped out, twisting and screaming as much as I could until Mark and whoever the fuck else was there stopped touching me. It took a while, but he eventually untied me because he was worried his neighbors would hear me yelling. He told me I was overreacting and that I didn't feel what I felt."

"Zo," I whisper, my eyes filled with tears. "That's horrible."

"When he took off the blindfold, there was no one else in the room, Lou."

"You felt what you felt."

"I keep going over it in my head, and I know there were more than two hands on my body. I know it deep in my bones."

The floor creaks, and I glance over my shoulder, finding Oliver filling the entrance to the living room.

Zoey stares at me with pleading eyes, the same ones she used to give me when we got in trouble and she didn't want me to throw her under the bus.

"Who is he, and where does he live?" Oliver asks without wanting to know the details.

Zoey's eyes slide to him before I glance over my shoulder to where he's standing. "Mark lives a few blocks over."

"Address?" he asks, his fists already curled at his sides.

"He lives in Riverfront Towers."

"Unit number?"

I stare back at my sister. "Tell him."

"But…"

"Zoey, honey." I hold her hands tightly, wishing I could take away all her memories of this awful night. "Tell Oliver. Let him handle Mark. Don't protect him."

"I don't want Oliver to get in trouble," she says to me.

Oliver's already pulling on his boots. "Men like him deserve all the hurt that's coming to them. Don't worry about me, doll. What's the unit?"

"Six-oh-seven," my sister says, always saying "oh" instead of zero. "But I don't think he's alone."

"I heard, and I'm about to find out that information for you and make sure Mark never even wants to lay eyes on you again."

"Do you want to call the cops instead, Zo?" I ask, wanting her to have the option of what she wants to do.

She shakes her head. "I don't want anyone to know."

"No one will," Oliver replies before I have a chance. He stalks toward me and kisses the top of my head. "You take care of her, and I'll take care of him."

I peer up at him, searching his eyes for reassurance. "Be safe."

"Sweetheart, Mark doesn't stand a chance."

And based on the size of Oliver, I know what he is saying is true. He is about to wipe the floor with Mark's ass.

"Don't kill him," I tell him.

"I'll leave him and whoever else is there breathing."

"I don't want you to end up in jail, Oli," I reply.

"I won't," he promises before the front door opens, and he's gone.

"I want a shower," Zoey says as soon as we're alone. "I need to scrub my skin."

"Whatever you want, sissy."

She nearly throws herself at me, wrapping her arms tightly around my neck. "I love you," she whispers against my hair.

"I love you too."

"You have a good man there, Lu."

"I think he's a keeper," I tell her, and my stomach flips the same way it did earlier when he got to my place, but for very different reasons.

Two hours pass, and I'm standing at the big window in the living room, staring at the street for any signs of Oliver. He texted me a half hour ago saying he was on his way back, but it's been radio silence since then.

I've never been as relieved as I was to get his text.

I had faith that Oliver could handle Mark and whoever else was there with him, but that didn't mean a small part of me didn't think the worst could happen even if the possibility was small.

The road glistens from the thick layer of ice that fell earlier in the night. The snow is coming down fast but has had no time to accumulate in one spot because the wind is whipping it everywhere except for where it has fallen.

Zoey passed out in the guest room an hour ago after a shower and three shots of tequila. She said it was the only way she'd be able to keep her eyes closed, and I didn't have a problem with her getting hammered and passing out. It's probably what I would've done in her situation, too.

My heart leaps as truck lights illuminate the virtual ice rink outside my house. He is here. He's back. I nearly hold my breath as he parks and climbs out, studying his movements carefully to see if he is hurt.

But Oliver being Oliver, he hops down from his truck, his strides sure and strong with his head held high. He looks more like he ran to the corner store to grab some milk than just kicked two full-grown men's asses after being awakened in the middle of the night.

I rush to the door as he gets closer to the house. I'm nearly vibrating off the floor with all the adrenaline running through my body. When his footsteps are closer, I open the door and soak him in.

His lip is bloodied, and one eye looks like it's beginning to swell. "It's done," he says as he stalks inside, shivering as he steps inside the warm foyer.

"Are you okay?" I ask, taking his coat from him as soon as he starts to shrug it off.

"I'm good, but they aren't."

"There were two?" I ask, but I already knew there were. Zoey's mind wasn't playing tricks on her. We all knew it, but I had hoped there was a chance because it could've been less traumatizing in the long run.

"Yep. Mark and his brother. Sick, twisted fuckers," Oliver says as he pulls off his boots and sets them to the side near the door.

Before he can stand fully upright, I fling myself at him, wrapping my arms around his shoulders. "Thank you," I breathe into the cold skin at his neck. "Thank you."

He's quick to snake his arms around my body, holding me so tight I think nothing in the world could ever hurt me. "They're going to be eating out of straws for a long time, sweetheart. I didn't want to leave them alive, but I also knew I didn't want to go to prison right now."

"Right now?"

"Well, never. That's Liam's thing, not mine. But the need for me to stop them from breathing and doing that shit to another woman was so strong, I almost let it overtake me."

"I don't want you in prison either," I tell him. "As

much as I want that bastard dead, I don't want it to be at the expense of your life."

"We're on the same page with that one."

I peer up at him, wondering how I got so lucky to find him. "Thank you," I say again, because once isn't enough. I don't know if there is enough time left in my short life to say it as much as he deserves.

His fingers find my chin as he cradles my face between his thumb and index finger. "No one hurts my girl or the ones she loves."

My insides hum at the statement. No one besides my family has ever had my back like that. Not a single man I ever dated gave a rat's ass about what happened to the people around me, and I hadn't been sure I'd ever find someone who did.

"What's yours is mine, and that makes their happiness and hurt mine too," he says.

I could love this man. I am falling for him—and falling hard. Who says things like that? No one I've ever known until Oliver entered my world. Not because he beat up two people tonight because of what they did to my sister, but because he cares enough about my happiness and the safety of those I love that he'll do anything to protect us and destroy anyone who does us harm.

CHAPTER 8
OLIVER

"I'M BACK, FUCKER," Liam says as he walks into the garage with a pep to his step. "I needed that."

I stare at him from behind my desk, wishing his trip had been a few days longer. "You look refreshed."

It's been nice without him here. Quieter. I love my brother even though he can be a complete shithead, but the amount of time his mouth is moving is way too much for me. It's not like he has anything important to say either. He talks to talk, and it's usually about bullshit.

"Vegas will do that to a man," he says, dropping down into his desk chair and stretching his arms wide. "The city's changed so much, but it's better than ever."

"I assume you won. You're in way too good of a mood to have lost your ass."

"You know it." He grabs a stack of papers on his

desk and starts to riffle through them. "Did I miss anything?"

I shake my head and grunt.

"Three days wasn't long enough."

"Suppose not," I grumble, knowing it was too short for me. I could've gone a few more days with as much peace and quiet as I could get at the garage.

"And what about the pretty girl?"

My eyes narrow on him. "What about her?"

"Did you see her again?"

"Yeah."

He raises an eyebrow as his fingers move through his beard like he's deep in contemplation. "Expound."

"Big word for you, brother. Did you read a dictionary on the plane?"

"Asshole," he mutters. "What happened with the chick?"

"The woman," I correct him, trying my best to keep the snarl out of my voice. "Saw her the other night."

"And?"

"Had dinner and fixed her dishwasher."

"Dishwasher?"

"Yeah, you know," I say, twirling my fingers in the air, being a sarcastic prick, "it washes dishes, and most people, unlike you, have one in their kitchen."

"You seeing her again?"

"Yep."

"When?"

I shrug, refusing to give him any details. My private life is just that…private. I would tell a stranger before I told Liam anything, especially about a woman I am seeing.

"She finish the work here?"

"Nope."

"Why not?"

"Because it's an unorganized shithole."

"You sleep with her yet?"

My jaw tightens as I stare at my brother, wishing he'd turn around and get right back on another plane. "Why?"

He chuckles and waves a hand at me. "You did."

"None of your business."

"I'd bet money you got laid recently. You're way too cheerful today. Not like your usual moody self."

I give him the middle finger and go back to staring at my computer screen instead of his smug face.

A police cruiser pulls up outside the open bay, and my brother's face drains of all its color.

"Shit," he whispers as his posture stiffens. "What the hell do they want?"

"You already broke the law? You've been back less than twenty-four hours."

He shakes his head. "I've been good lately."

Lately is the operative word. There's a list a mile long of shit Liam's done in his life that could make this visit possible.

Two officers climb out, one male and one female.

Their eyes roam their surroundings, taking in every possible threat.

"Good morning, officers," I say, not bothering to get up from my desk. "What can we help you with?"

The female tips her head in my direction, but there's no smile on her face. "We're looking for Oliver Winston."

My stomach plummets like I've been hurled down the tallest roller coaster hill.

"Ooooh," my brother says as his lips turn up in a sadistic smile. "Not me." He raises his hands, looking more than a little excited that this call has nothing to do with his history of every type of illegal thing.

"I'm Oliver," I tell them as my gaze moves from her to her partner. "What's wrong?"

The male officer blows out a breath as his hand drops to his belt, which is never a good sign. "We're here about an incident that happened the other night."

My mind drifts back, and I know exactly what this is about. "Okay," I say, playing clueless and hoping that my intuition is right.

"We have a victim who claims you came to his apartment and assaulted him."

My brother gasps, drawing my attention, along with that of the two officers.

"What in the world…"

"Zip it, Liam," I say through gritted teeth, not needing his brand of bullshit today. "And?"

"He's pressing charges, but we wanted to bring you down to the station to get your side of the story, take a statement."

"Are you arresting me?" I ask them, shockingly calm in this situation.

The woman glances down before she looks me in the eye. "We'd like to take you downtown."

"We are downtown," my brother interrupts, stirring the pot in a moment that calls for him to keep his mouth closed.

"Can I come down after work?"

The male officer shakes his head. "No. Sorry, sir, but this needs to be done now."

"Can I take my own car?"

"No, sir," the female says.

"Busted," my brother teases, and it takes everything in me not to launch myself across the space separating our desks and adding another charge to what I'm sure is a list from the incident with Mark. "Fuck, I never thought I'd see the day."

"Fine," I say, pushing myself up from the desk and glancing toward my brother. "Call Hal."

He nods. "On it," he says, grabbing his phone and peeling away from the office area, heading toward the bank of cabinets in the back of the garage.

The female cop takes a step forward. "Leave everything," she says to me as she reaches for her handcuffs.

"So, you are arresting me?"

"It's a safety precaution," she replies.

I growl, wishing I could get my hands around Mark's neck again. "Fine," I say with my jaw clenched so tight, I'm surprised I don't break a tooth.

I turn around, placing my hands behind my back to make their job easier. Do I deserve to be in handcuffs? No. Did I beat the living shit out of Mark and leave him in a puddle of his own blood? Absolutely. I'd do it again too. A man like him deserved worse than I gave him. He is lucky to be alive.

"You have the right to remain silent…" the officer says, and I tune her out.

I have to believe this will all get sorted out downtown once I am able to explain my side of the story. There has to be justice in this world, and I am on the side of good, while Mark represents everything bad, deserving eating through a straw for the next six months.

"Mr. Winston, I'm Officer Williams." The man sits down across from me as I'm handcuffed to the steel table that's no doubt bolted to the floor. "I'm here for your statement."

My statement? That's laughable. "I want my lawyer," I tell him, knowing my rights.

"He'll be here soon," he says, placing his pen

down on a blank form between us. "But I thought we could talk first about what happened the other night with the victim."

I let out a bitter laugh. Mark's no victim, and if I had to hazard a guess, he is the one who has a string of victims probably strewn across the Chicago metro area. Each one of them too scared to come forward, fearing no one would believe them, which is most likely true, no matter how sad that shit is.

"He was pretty beat up. To me, it looks to be personal and not random."

Give the man a door prize. He surmised that from the injuries. Anyone could do that shit. You don't need to be a beat cop or a detective to put two and two together.

I would bet my life that Mark didn't tell them why I kicked his ass, and for now, I'm not about to tell them either.

It isn't my place.

I'm not his victim, and if Zoey wants that shit locked down tight, I'll lock it down. I'll serve whatever stupid-ass jail time they want to give me because men like Mark don't even deserve to breathe.

"Lawyer," I say again, drawing the word out super slowly and spending a particularly long time on the letter R. I rub my fingers together, feeling the sticky residue of the ink they used for fingerprinting as I glare at the man.

He ignores my request this time. "Was there a specific reason you attacked Mr. Jones?"

I stare at Officer Williams and keep my mouth shut. My brother always hammered that shit into my head. Giving any answer to any question is a no-no. It could be the best answer, and the cops would find a way to twist that shit into the worst.

"Mr. Jones's injuries were extensive. He has a broken arm, a concussion, a broken jaw, a broken nose, and three broken fingers."

My only regret is that I didn't break all ten, but I am not about to tell the cop that.

I don't make a sound, only stare.

"He's still in the hospital after the surgery to have his jaw wired shut."

Sucks for him, but that doesn't mean that I'm not happy about his suffering because I damn well am.

"We have a written statement from the victim because he's unable to talk. He claims he'd never seen you before that night and had no idea why you would attack him."

I only wish I'd fucking made his dick unusable so he wouldn't have the ability to violate someone in the same way he did Zoey. That is my only regret about the entire shitshow.

The door to the interview room opens, and a man pops his head inside. "Lawyer's here."

"Damn it," Officer Williams mutters as he scoops up the papers in front of us. "I'll be back."

I turn my head in his direction as he walks toward the door, knowing this isn't over, even if Hal is here to try to save the day.

Hal steps into the room a moment later, takes the seat across from me, and holds up a finger.

I follow his lead, remaining silent. I've never been in this position before. This is my brother's life, never mine. Well, at least not until now.

A good minute later, Hal finally opens his mouth, "I never thought I'd get that call."

"Makes two of us."

"What happened?"

I glance around, wondering if anyone is listening.

"Attorney-client privilege. They can't listen."

I sigh and ease back into my chair with my arms in front of me, still cuffed to the damn table. "The asshole took part in an assault on one of my friends."

"What kind of assault?"

"She's female," I tell him.

Hal clucks his tongue as he nods. "Got it."

"She was terrified, and I thought I'd teach Mark a lesson so it doesn't happen to her again."

He whistles as he opens a manila folder that has a few photos of a very black-and-blue face that's way beyond swollen. "And boy, did you."

"What are we looking at here? How long in jail?"

Hal rubs his jawline as he stares at me. "Would this woman be willing to testify?"

"I won't ask her. It's a no, Hal. She's been through enough shit."

"Understood." His fingers move a little faster over his skin. "It's your first offense. Clean record. The judge could be more lenient due to your military service, and I could work with the DA to see if we could get your charges reduced. Maybe six months if we're lucky."

That answer hits me like a ton of bricks.

He lifts his hand to his head, straightening his awful combover. The man wouldn't look half bad if he'd just shave his dome instead of trying to pass it off like he still has hair where he clearly doesn't. "Maybe four if we get really lucky."

"Whatever," I mutter, knowing I did what I did, and if I have to do the time to keep Zoey from having to tell the world about what happened to her, I'll do it. "Make it happen. Cut a deal."

"I'll get your bail posted and get to work on everything, but I'll make it happen."

"Work miracles, Hal."

"I'll do my best, Oliver. I hate seeing you like this."

"Shit happens, and I'd do it all over again, given half the chance."

"Men like him deserve everything they get. Hang tight."

I lift my hands the three inches I'm able to. "Not going anywhere, Hal."

He gives me a sad smile and shakes his head. "They're ridiculous."

That's one word for the Chicago PD. They are doing their job, but that doesn't mean they are on the right side of this. They aren't, but I could never tell them that. I'll forever be the bad guy, and my spotless record no longer exists. It doesn't matter. It isn't like my job depends on any of that shit. I own my own business, and if I have an arrest, it's not like I am going to fire myself.

Time ticks by slower than it ever has in my entire life. Minutes feel like hours, and hours feel like days. I wait and wait some more for someone to get me out of here, and right when I am about to give up hope, the door to the interview room opens again.

"Bail's been posted," Officer Williams says as he walks in, holding a set of keys in his hand. "But I have a feeling we'll be talking again soon."

"Doubtful," I mumble as he unlocks the cuffs, and I immediately rub my wrists, relishing the feeling of their freedom.

I follow Officer Williams out of the room, down a long and depressing hallway to the front of the station. Hal is waiting in a plastic chair, holding the same folder that has the pictures of Mark's face and what I did to it.

"Ready?" he asks as he rises to his feet.

"Yep."

"Need to get anything?" he asks, glancing toward the police officer at the desk.

"Got nothing," I tell him because I left everything, including my phone and wallet, back at the garage. No point in bringing anything with me when I knew they'd take it away once we got here.

"Your brother's outside waiting for you."

"Great," I grumble, knowing my shitty day isn't going to get better any time soon.

"He's in a surprisingly good mood," Hal says to me as he pushes open the door to the police station and sunlight streams into the small corridor.

"He's enjoying my arrest."

Hal chuckles. "Something like that."

"Brother," Liam says, pushing his entire body off the tow truck parked right outside the station and in a no-parking fire zone. Dummy. "Welcome to freedom."

"Shut up," I tell him.

"I'll be in touch," Hal says, tipping his head at my brother. "Liam."

"Hal," Liam says, giving him a smile. "Nice not to be on the other side today."

"Miracles do happen," Hal says, stalking away from us like his ass is on fire.

"Where to?" Liam asks as he rounds the front of the truck.

"The garage," I tell him, wanting nothing more than to go back to work and forget this entire shitty day ever happened.

"So, you ever going to tell me what happened?" he asks as soon as we're both inside the truck and a block away from the station.

"No."

"Damn, brother. Tell me. I'm not going to say shit. What made you snap? You're always so calm."

"He hurt someone who didn't deserve it."

"The girl?" he asks, and I know he's talking about Lulu.

"No, but someone close to her. He deserved everything I gave him and more, brother."

Liam sucks in a breath between his teeth. "Probably. Men like that always do. She okay?"

"Who?" I ask, my mind elsewhere as the city streets blur by.

"Lulu's girl."

I nod. "Physically, yes. But mentally, I don't know."

"Shitty people out there, man. Shitty people. What did Hal say?"

"Best case is four."

"Four what?" Liam rolls to a stop at a light and turns his gaze toward me. "Days?"

"Months."

Liam's eyes widen. "What? That's insane."

I shrug. "I did a lot of damage."

"Sounds like he is the one who deserves to be behind bars for four months, not you. What the hell am I going to do if you're gone?"

"Take care of the garage. You're a big boy."

"You're the responsible one."

"Fuck. I know. Don't let it all fall to shit, so when I get out, I beat your ass and wind up right back behind bars again."

Liam laughs. "It ain't gonna happen."

"What?"

"You're not going for four months. Hal will work his magic. You wait and see. I can't have you gone for four months. I can't. I'm too much of a fuckup for all that responsibility."

"From your lips to God's ears," I whisper. "I know Hal's good, but I don't think he can work that kind of miracle."

"He can."

My brother is more hopeful than I am, but he has far more experience with our criminal justice system than I do. Maybe he is right. Maybe I will get off with a slap on the wrist, but that would take the biggest miracle of my life and a hell of a lot of skill on Hal's part. He is a great lawyer, but sometimes that isn't enough.

But I have a bigger worry.

Time inside doesn't bother me. If my brother could survive, I know I could too.

My biggest problem will be telling Lulu what happened and that I'll be gone before we have a chance to really get going.

CHAPTER 9
LULU

"HEY, kid. What's the face for?" my uncle Vinnie asks as he slides into the booth across from me.

I turn my face toward him and away from the window facing the street. "Something's wrong with the guy I'm seeing."

"Break up with him," he says quickly, without even a moment to think of anything else. "If he's already a problem, he'll always be one."

I smile at my uncle, loving that he's forever trying to look out for me. "He's not a problem, Unc, but there is something wrong. He called and wanted to talk to me, and I could tell by the tone of his voice that something's wrong, and I don't know what it could be."

My uncle blinks at me a few times like he's processing all the words I just said. Hell, it would take me a minute or two too, if I hadn't been the one who said them.

"When do you talk to him about whatever is wrong?" he asks, being patient with me like he always is.

People would think that my uncle would be the impatient type. He's an ex-pro footballer and one of the most well-known players in Chicago. There are people who come to the bar on the off chance they'll get to meet the great Vinnie Gallo, quarterback and football savior of the Windy City. But to me, he's my uncle, and he's a sweet man who only wants the best for his family and friends.

"He's on his way here."

"I'll stick around in case I need to kick his ass."

I laugh as soon as the words come out of his mouth, trying to picture Oliver and my uncle going at it. "That's unnecessary."

"Why?" he asks, tilting his head and staring at me like I'm off my rocker.

"He's nice. You're nice."

"We're men, Lulu. We're all shitheads."

"You're not a shithead," I say, thinking back on all my great memories with my uncle when I was growing up.

"Wait. Which guy is this?" He makes it sound like I have a ton of men in my life who are dying to date me.

"Oliver."

"The one who saved your life?"

Of course word has already spread around the family about Oliver's heroic act. "That's the one."

"He's only half a shithead, then," Uncle Vinnie says.

The loud rumble of an engine draws my attention back to the street. It's Oliver. My stomach twists as he cuts the engine and climbs out, looking so damn sexy from my position.

"That him?"

I nod slowly without looking at my uncle. "It is."

"A man his size missed his calling. He should've been a football player," he says, always looking at everyone from a sports angle.

He keeps talking, but I can't reply. I don't have the bandwidth because I'm too busy staring at Oliver's face, trying to decipher what the problem is before he walks inside.

"I'll go so you two can talk, but I'm sticking nearby in case you need me to handle him."

"What?" I ask, looking at my uncle once Oliver is out of view, heading toward the entrance to the bar.

He slides out of the booth and stands at the end of the table, his fingers pressed against the wood top. "I'm here if you need me. I won't leave until I know you're okay."

"Thanks," I say, my voice soft and my throat dry. I pull my hands into my lap, twisting my fingers together to do something to keep myself from a complete panic attack.

The door to the bar opens as my uncle walks away, leaving me to have whatever this conversation is with Oliver alone. My eyes lock with Oliver's, and I wave, not even bothering to stand from my seat. I can't. I think my entire body would shake from nerves. Oliver doesn't stress me out, but I could tell when he called that something big had happened and he wanted to talk to me as soon as possible about it.

"Hey," he says once he makes it to the table where my ass is virtually superglued to the seat. He bends forward, his hand touching my face as he kisses my cheek. "You're a sight for sore eyes, sweetheart."

"Hey, handsome." I stare up at him, seeing the storm raging in his eyes. "Are you okay?"

"I'm better now," he says as he takes the seat my uncle just vacated.

"What's wrong?"

He scrubs a hand down his face before his fingertips disappear into his beard. "I ran into an issue today."

"Okay," I reply, drawing out the word. I twist my fingers faster in my lap as the knot in my stomach tightens.

"Mark is a problem."

"Mark?" I ask, trying to think of who the hell Mark is, when the name suddenly slams into me like a ton of bricks. My body goes cold.

"Yeah, that one," he says as the color leaves my cheeks.

"What happened?"

He places one hand on the table, kneading his fingertips into the wood. "Don't freak out."

I suck in a deep breath as my body goes rigid. My heart, which was already beating at a frantic pace, picks up speed. Nothing good starts with that statement. Nothing.

He glances down at the table. "The cops came to the garage."

My chest tightens as my heart feels like it's battering the backs of my ribs and is liable to burst free. "Oh no," I whisper as I place one of my hands near his on the table, my pinkie touching his.

"He went to the cops, and they arrested me," he says, finally bringing his gaze back to mine. "But I have a lawyer working on everything."

My head starts to spin, and my vision goes blurry as I breathe faster than any human probably should. "Fuck," I whisper, feeling the world go fuzzy.

"Lulu," Oliver calls out as everything goes white and there's only nothingness around me.

When my eyes flutter open again, I'm in warm arms and I'm comfortable. I blink up at Oliver, who's staring down at me with softness dotting his features. "Sweetheart," he whispers. "Breathe, baby."

"I had the worst dream," I say, trying to lift myself up from the awkward position I'm in.

But then it hits me. It wasn't a dream. I'm at the bar. I'm here with Oliver. Everything comes crashing into me again. All his words. The statement about the cops. His arrest. Mark.

"Fuck," I hiss as I sit up quickly, my head spinning again.

"Easy," Oliver says to me softly.

"Here's some water," Uncle Vinnie says. "Good, she's awake."

I turn my glassy gaze toward my uncle, but I can't find the words. My head's too busy trying to process everything Oliver said, even if it was only a few sentences.

"What happened?" Uncle Vinnie asks as he takes the spot across from us while Oliver stays by my side, moving the glass of water in front of me.

"I didn't eat today," I lie.

Zoey doesn't want anyone to know what happened. I wouldn't either. And there's no way Uncle Vinnie can know why Oliver beat up Mark because it'll spread through the family like a brush fire during a drought. And once everyone knows, they'll go after Mark too, and they'll be arrested just like Oliver.

"Entirely my fault. I know not to do that."

Uncle Vinnie eyes me. The man can smell bullshit a mile away, and I am awful at lying. Without missing a beat, my uncle turns his skeptical gaze toward Oliver.

"You going to be honest with me or bullshit me like my niece?" he asks Oliver point-blank. "What had her pass out cold when she was fine a minute ago?"

Oliver peers over at me, and I do my best to convey to him to keep his mouth shut. But I don't have ESP, and this is a time when it would be absolutely useful. My fingers tighten on the sleeve of his jacket, holding on to him like my very life depends on the connection.

This is bad.

So very bad.

He was arrested.

Arrest leads to court. Court leads to jail. Jail leads to Oliver being gone for however long the judge feels is necessary for the crime that wasn't a crime that Oliver supposedly committed.

Shit.

This is my fault. He wouldn't have gone to Mark's place if he hadn't overheard my conversation with Zoey.

We caused this problem for him.

A week ago, he was living his best life without our issues. He wasn't facing jail time for something that had nothing to do with him.

"A man was a problem for a woman in this family, and I took care of him, if you know what I mean," Oliver starts to explain, doing his best not to give too many details, which is impressive.

I couldn't have done a better job myself, and I am adept at giving as little information as possible.

"Go on," Uncle Vinnie says with a lift of his chin in Oliver's direction.

"The asshole went to the cops, and I was arrested because the guy is a dick."

"Which woman?" my uncle asks with a raised eyebrow as his gaze slides in my direction.

"Not me," I say quickly, but I don't say anything more. "And it's not important who because Oliver handled it."

"He handled it, but now it's coming back to bite him in the ass, Lou. You have a lawyer?" Uncle Vinnie asks Oliver.

Oliver nods. "He came to the station and bailed me out. He's working on a deal right now to save me some jail time."

"What kind of time are we talking?" Uncle Vinnie asks.

"Under a year if I'm lucky," Oliver says like he's ordering a pizza or talking about the weather and not how many months of his life he'll lose because of something that was done to a member of my family and not directly to him.

His words play on repeat in my head as I sit next to Oliver, finally feeling numb.

Uncle Vinnie whistles as he shakes his head. "That's a fucking lot. How badly did you handle him?"

"I broke lots of shit, but he deserved it."

"No doubt," Uncle Vinnie says with a nod. He's awfully calm about the entire conversation, which is like him, but under the circumstances, not like him at all. "And who did this guy do something to?"

My family never can let shit go, and neither will Uncle Vinnie. I know that deep in my soul, but that doesn't mean I will give up the information willingly without Zoey's consent.

"It doesn't matter," Oliver says. "I'd do it for anyone in this family."

Uncle Vinnie's lips turn up ever so slightly. "Good to know. Who's the lawyer?"

"Hal Bloom."

Uncle Vinnie's lips twist. "I don't know him."

"He has his own office. He's my brother's lawyer. I've never needed one except for business stuff, but Hal assures me he can work out a deal so I don't have to do a longer stint inside."

A stint inside. I never thought I'd be with a man who uttered those words. But here I am, and I am proud of Oliver, even if he did something most people would abhor. He did it for the right reasons, and I'll forever be grateful to him for having Zoey's back at a time she felt violated and helpless.

"I have some friends in the DA's office. I'll place some calls," Uncle Vinnie tells Oliver.

"Totally unnecessary," Oliver grumbles. "Hal will handle it."

"You seem like a good guy, Oliver. You did right by my family even if you won't tell me who you were protecting." Uncle Vinnie's gaze slides to me, and I look away. I'm not saying shit, and he knows it. "But sometimes the criminal justice system has less to do with justice and more to do with who you know. I'll poke around and see what I can do."

"Thank you," I say to my uncle, but I'm still unable to meet his stare because I don't want to break.

Oliver reaches over and intertwines his fingers with mine. "I appreciate the offer, but I'm not sure you can change the course of events. I messed him up pretty bad."

"Did he deserve it?"

"Completely," Oliver replies.

"Never hurts to try. I wouldn't be able to sleep at night if I didn't at least make a few phone calls. You saved my niece's life and helped someone else I love, even if I don't know who they are."

I swallow roughly and seal my lips shut.

Vinnie taps the table with his index finger. "I'll be in touch," he says before sliding back out of the booth, leaving us alone.

"This is bad," I whisper, staring down at where our hands are connected and resting on my leg. "So bad."

"Hey," Oliver whispers, squeezing my hand.

"The worst."

"Lou," Oliver says, placing the fingers of his free hand under my chin and forcing my eyes upward to meet his. "Look at me, sweetheart."

Tears sting the corners of my eyes. He's so sweet and gentle with me, and my heart can barely handle any more. I should be comforting him. He's the one who's about to lose his freedom for something he never would've been involved in if it weren't for me and my family dropping into his life out of nowhere.

"It's my fault."

Oliver strokes my chin with his thumb. "Baby, look at me."

I let out a deep breath I didn't know I was holding and finally drag my gaze to his. "You wouldn't be in this trouble if it weren't for us."

"I'd do it all again, even knowing what I know now and facing jail time."

My mouth drops open. "How can you say that? Jail is jail, Oli."

A small, sad smile forms on his lips. "I'd do anything to keep you and the ones you love safe, Lulu. A few months away is worth it to know that shithead will never do that to Zoey or another woman again."

"A few months inside?" I ask as my body stiffens. "A few months inside? A few months inside?" My voice rises with each repetition. "It's more than a few months inside. It's a record. It's your freedom. It's your life."

Oliver pulls me against him, holding me so tightly

the only thing I feel is his warm strength. "It'll be okay, Lulu. I need you to calm down and breathe."

"I'm breathing, and I'm freaking out," I say as I sag against him, pulling in a deep breath as loudly and dramatically as I can so he'll stop telling me to breathe.

He tightens his hold as he places his mouth near my ear. "If I go inside, I don't expect you to wait around for me."

I shiver at the deepness of his voice as the anger from his words ignites my insides. "Don't be an asshole."

"I'm not being an asshole, sweetheart. I don't want your world to stop turning, even if mine does."

CHAPTER 10
OLIVER

I DIDN'T THINK things could go from bad to worse, but it all happened so fast, I don't even have time to brace myself.

Lulu's father slides into the booth next to her, ignoring me entirely. "What's wrong? Vinnie called."

Lulu turns her gaze toward her uncle, who's sitting at the bar, looking in the other direction. He has to feel the daggers she is throwing in his direction with her eyes.

"Hey. I'm here, not there," her dad says to her.

I shift, the pleather underneath my ass squeaking. "Sorry," I mutter, but no one's paying any attention to me.

"What happened?" he asks Lulu again when she doesn't answer. "He said I needed to drop everything and bring my ass down here. So, I'm here, and I want to know what's wrong."

"Dad," Lulu says softly. "Nothing's wrong with me."

"Well, there's something."

Lulu's eyes move in my direction. "Oliver got in trouble for something we caused."

"We?" he asks, skipping over the trouble bit.

"Me and…" Her eyes snap to his again, and she pinches her lips closed.

"Who?"

Lulu shakes her head.

"Lulu."

"I promised I wouldn't tell," she whispers.

Her father grunts as his one hand that's been resting on the table curls closed. "Fine," he says, but his voice is tight and higher than before. "What kind of trouble are we talking about?"

"A small stint inside," I answer, wanting to take the pressure off her.

His head turns toward me so slowly that if I were a kid, I would've shit my pants. "Jail?" he asks.

"Prison's more likely," Lulu says before slapping her hand over her mouth as her eyes widen.

"What in the hell did you do?" he asks me.

I lean back, sliding my arm across the top of the booth, and try to pretend to be relaxed. "I may have gotten carried away."

He tilts his head as his jaw ticks upward. "You think?"

"I didn't have a choice. Someone needed to learn a lesson, and I was the one to teach it."

It is all as simple as that. Men like that deserve to be put down, and I got as close as I could without landing the final blow. Even if I didn't end his life, I know two things for certain—he won't talk to Zoey again, and he'll think twice before doing that to anyone else.

Her dad, Lucio, a man I've met once, blows a long, deep breath as he glares at me. "And who decided it was your place?"

"No decision needed to be made. I was there. It was that simple."

I'm not winning any points with him, but I don't think there is anything I could say that would make him understand. I'll *never* be able to make him understand without any details. It is impossible since Zoey doesn't want anyone to know, and Lulu isn't even willing to say anything.

"Dad, I can't give you all the details, but someone I love was hurt by them. Oliver was there, overheard everything, and decided to act so that piece of shit didn't hurt them again."

"Is it someone I know?"

"Maybe," Lulu whispers before she grimaces.

"I'll take that as a yes. How did they hurt them?"

"You don't want to know," Lulu replies.

Lucio grits his teeth so hard, they squeak. "How

bad did you hurt him?" Lucio asks me, already piecing shit together.

"He's in the hospital," I answer.

"Good," Lucio says. "He deserves worse."

"He does," I say.

"They arrest you already?"

I nod. "Just got out on bail."

"How long are they talking?"

"A year or less," I tell him. "Hopefully the less side of it."

Lulu drops her face into the palms of her hands. "This is so bad. I feel so awful."

Her father reaches over, clasping her forearm. "Baby, shit happens. It's not your fault."

"It's not, Lou. I didn't have to do what I did, but I did it and I'd do it again to keep you and them safe," I add.

"We'll figure this out," her father tells her. "It won't be that bad."

Sure, it won't be that bad for them. I'll be the one on the inside of a cell, nothing but bars and criminals around me. Their life will go on as usual, no matter how long I'm sent away. But I know, every day I would be gone, Lulu would be riddled with guilt, blaming herself for something she didn't even do wrong.

"I know someone who might be able to help," Lucio says, grabbing his phone off the table.

"Who?" Lulu asks him, trying to catch a glimpse of his screen.

"Pop, come downstairs to the bar," he says to the person on the other end of the call before he sets his phone back down.

"You called Grandpa?" Lulu asks with wide eyes. "Why did you call Grandpa?"

"You know his past, and if anyone knows anyone who can help, it's him."

"I have a lawyer," I tell him, wanting him to know I don't need any help. I've got this covered.

Lucio chuckles with a shake of his head. "We're looking for other avenues, and if there is one, my dad will know it."

"Huh," I mutter, letting that statement replay in my mind. I'm not about to turn down help. Anything that can be done to keep me from going to the big house for months on end, I am more than willing to try.

"Grandpa is going to have so many questions," Lulu tells her dad.

"We'll keep the details brief," Lucio explains, as if it'll be that easy. It wasn't with him, but somehow Lulu remained tight-lipped about her sister, keeping the secret when many would've spilled every detail.

"I'm here," an older man says, stalking through the dining room from the area behind the bar. "I was in the middle of a nice snack and my favorite show, so this better be good." His gaze moves from

Lucio to Lulu and then to me. "I already know it's not."

"Hi, Grandpa," Lulu says with a little wave and a halfhearted smile that doesn't make her eyes sparkle.

"Hey, kiddo. What's wrong?"

Lucio tips his head in my direction. "Lulu's friend here got into some trouble and is looking at possibly a year inside."

The old man sucks in a breath as his eyebrows shoot up so fast, and I would have been pretty sure nothing else on his aging frame moved that quick anymore. "Wowsers," he says. "That's not a short stint."

I shake my head. "Don't I know it."

"Scooch," he says to me, motioning for me to move my ass across the bench, and without a moment's hesitation, I move. "You been processed?"

"Arrested and out on bail."

"Good. Good."

I don't know how in the world any of that is good, but if he says it, I have to believe him. The man looks like he's been through some things. Lucio said the man had a past, and I am fairly certain much of it isn't good.

"Lawyer?" he asks.

"Yes."

"Good. Now, tell me what happened."

I spend the next ninety seconds explaining as much as I can without giving away Zoey's name or any identifying details so her grandpa and dad can't piece shit together. When I finish explaining, Lulu exhales and her shoulders sag. She was wound so tight, assuming I'd slip up and the two guys would figure out it was Zoey I'd protected.

"Vin, grab a paper and pen for me from behind the bar," her grandfather calls out.

Her uncle Vinnie moves quickly, snapping up a pen and paper that are lying nearby. "Are we making a plan?" Vinnie asks as he carries over the two items and places them in front of his father. "Because whatever it is, I'm in."

"You're not in," Lucio tells him. "I'm not in either. We're leaving this one up to Pops."

Vinnie jerks his head back, looking at his brother like he has three heads. "Are you feeling okay today?"

"I'm fine," Lucio snaps.

"This is Dad we're talking about," Vinnie adds.

"I'm right here," the older man says, sliding the pen and paper in front of me on the table. "I need your details and the lawyer's information. I'll handle the rest from there."

"What happened?" Vinnie asks, staring down at the entire table like we're all bananas.

I stay out of their conversation, finding it easier to write down the information than wade into a family discussion. If I keep talking, I'll slip up eventually and give too much away.

"No time," her grandfather says, running a hand

through his wavy salt-and-pepper hair. "I got shit to do. It's time to work a miracle."

"Well then, you're screwed," Vinnie says, and I know those words are pointed at me.

"Have some faith in your old man," his father says to him. "I've been known to get out of a jam or two."

"Or fifty," Lucio adds.

I have absolutely no idea what's going on, but for some odd reason, I feel like her grandfather is being honest and earnest. "You've done this before?"

"Plenty."

Vinnie snorts. "My father's past is..."

"Colorful," Lucio says, finishing his brother's sentence.

"I know a lot of people in the business," her grandfather says.

"That's not a lie," Lucio says. "If anyone can help and make the entire thing disappear, it's him."

My eyebrows furrow as I stare at the older gentleman. He looks so kind and innocent, I'd never think he'd know how to get someone out of jail time. He looks more like the type of guy who'd be standing over the stove, making his famous meatball recipe.

"I'm sorry," Lulu says to me from her father's side. "I wish I'd never dragged you into this."

"I don't regret it," I tell her, staring her straight in the eyes. She's so damn pretty. Too pretty for me, really. But more than her beauty, it's her sweet silliness that has a choke hold on my cock. "I'd do it again if given the chance. I'll always do whatever it takes to protect you and your family, Lou."

It suddenly hits me that all three men are staring at me. I swallow, wishing I'd kept those words for later. They were a little too heartfelt for public consumption, but I don't think for a moment that they're looking down on me for what I did. At least not anymore, now that they know more of the story.

"Solid response," Vinnie says, tapping his finger against the table. "I approve."

"Not too bad," Lucio says, "but also a little too much."

"Dad, stop," Lulu says to her father. "Oliver is a nice guy."

"Obviously," her father replies. "Not many men would feel the same way he does. They'd be filled with regret when facing time behind bars for something that they didn't need to do."

"What kind of shit man wouldn't need to do anything when they saw someone in pain?" I ask.

"Plenty," her father answers. "And not a damn one would deserve to breathe the same air as her."

"I couldn't agree more," her grandfather says as he shoos his son away from the side of the booth. "I need to get on this ASAP."

Vinnie steps aside, letting his father get up. "The man has a fire under his ass."

"Even in retirement, I don't get much peace," her grandfather says as he stands and stretches.

"Someday, my old body will give out, and then what are you guys going to do?"

"Don't say that, Grandpa," Lulu tells him, her eyes carefully watching him as he moves.

I never knew my grandfather or grandmother on either side of my family. I can't imagine being as old as I am now and still being able to hold a conversation with them. I would give almost anything to spend a small amount of time with any of them to learn about my family's past and what makes me me.

"I'm not getting any younger, kiddo, but I'm not going anywhere yet except upstairs to make phone calls. Let me know if anything else happens," he says to me.

"I will," I promise him.

The door to the bar opens, and Zoey walks in, stiffening immediately as her eyes land on Lulu, me, Lucio, and Vinnie. I know what she's thinking immediately. We told them, but we didn't. I never would, and I know Lulu would rather go to her grave than tell Zoey's business.

"Hey, baby," Lucio says, waving over his younger daughter.

Fuck. This isn't good. If the man puts two and two together, he's going to lose his absolute shit.

"Hey, Daddy," Zoey says as she moves toward us at a slower pace than most people walk when excited to see someone. "What are you guys doing?" Her eyes move to me, and I do my best not to give anything away.

"Nothing, Zo. Oliver got himself into a bit of trouble."

Zoey's eyes flash with panic, and she nearly trips over her own feet.

"Nothing huge," Lulu says, trying to send signals to her sister to chill out. "I'll tell you about it later."

"What kind of trouble?" Zoey asks as I slide over, making a spot for her in the booth.

"He was arrested for getting into a fight," Lulu explains, doing her best to make it seem like Zoey's clueless about everything.

"Arrested?" Zoey's mouth hangs open as her gaze moves to me. "When?"

"This morning. It's not a big deal. It'll all get sorted."

"Fuck," she whispers as she squeezes her eyes shut. "That's awful."

"Grandpa's going to do his best to get him out of the jam," Lucio tells Zoey.

Zoey's eyes fly open and snap to her sister. "Oh my God. How many people know about this?"

"Just us," Lulu explains, "And only what they need to know, and that includes you." Lulu's trying to cover her tracks, but whether she knows it or not, she's failing.

Lucio's gaze is moving between the two of them, and I can see the wheels spinning. The man isn't dumb. He's been around these two for their entire lives. If anyone knows them and their code talk, it's their own father.

"No!" Lucio barks out, staring at Zoey. "You?"

"Me what?" Zoey asks, touching her chest and starting her backpedaling. "I didn't do anything."

"Was it you?" Lucio asks again, leaning over the table and taking his daughter's hand in his.

"What?" She's good, but she's white as a ghost, making it damn near impossible for him not to get all the confirmation he needs.

"What happened to you, baby?" he asks, but this time, his voice is gentle. "You know you can tell me anything."

"Daddy," she whispers, her gaze dropping to where their hands are connected. "I can't…"

"Was it you?" he asks again.

"Yes," she says, but her voice is so quiet, I can barely hear her.

"Fuck," he hisses, and the pain is etched all over his face as the reality of everything that could've happened slams into him. "Did he…"

"Dad, I don't want to talk about it, okay?" Zoey says, but this time, she's looking at his face, begging him for a reprieve. "I want to forget everything that happened. Please don't make me talk about it."

"I won't," he says as he sweeps his thumb across the back of her hand. "Are you okay?"

"I'm better than I was."

"What can I do?" he asks.

"Nothing, Daddy. Oliver did enough, and Lulu helped me too. I just need time."

I'm not sure time will make anything better. That type of betrayal and trauma isn't something that any length of hours or days can erase.

"Thank you," Lucio says.

I drag my gaze from Lulu to him, finding him staring at me. "For what?"

"For protecting my girls," he says.

"Always and forever."

CHAPTER 11
LULU

EVERYTHING IS A MESS.

Oliver is facing jail time. Sure, my grandfather said he'd do what he could, but the chances of him having the ability to make everything disappear are slim to none. Even with his past, he has only so many strings he can pull.

My dad figured out Zoey was the person we were protecting. I did my best not to spill Zoey's secret, but one look at her and he knew. He didn't probe too much after she said it was indeed her that Oliver had been protecting, but that doesn't mean he is content not to want to find out more. Do I think he'll let it drop? Absolutely not.

I stare out the window, standing in my living room in my favorite pair of fuzzy slippers. I curl my toes against the plush bottoms, grounding myself as I pull in a shaky breath.

A knock on the door makes me jump, and I whirl around as my heart pounds in my chest.

"Lulu, open up!" Zoey yells through the thick wood door as her knocking grows more frantic. "Lulu!"

I rush toward the door, almost tripping over my area rug that always has a corner curled up, no matter what I do to flatten it. "Shit," I call out, catching myself on the coffee table before I have the chance to face-plant into the hardwood floor. "Coming!"

"Lulu," Zoey groans like she didn't hear me tell her I am on my way to let her in.

When I fling the door open, Zoey almost falls forward like she'd been using her head to pound on my door. I catch her by the shoulders, pushing her upright. "What's wrong? What happened?" I ask, unable to keep the panic out of my voice.

"Everything's a mess," she whines as she places her head on my shoulder and wraps her arms around me. "It's my fault."

Oh no, she doesn't. She's not going to shoulder the blame for something a grown-ass vile man whom she trusted did to her.

I kick the door closed with my foot because my hands are trapped underneath my sister's arms. "Let's sit down and have a drink," I tell her, moving us across the room toward my couch. She's attached to me like a parasite, and it takes all my strength to walk with her extra weight.

She used to do this when we were little, but she was lighter then, and for some reason, I thought the behavior was cute. Now…not so much.

I lean over my plush couch until her hold on me loosens and she flops backward, fully detached from me. "Martini or margarita?"

"Martini," she says, staring up at me with tears in her eyes. "A sweet one."

My kind little sister. No one deserves what happened to her. Am I sad Oliver is facing jail time? Yes. Did the guy he beat the crap out of deserve it? Absolutely. If I'd known he was going to get arrested, would I have stopped him? I don't think there was any stopping him that night. He knew what the consequences of his actions could be. I did too, and there isn't a thing I'd do to change what happened after Zoey told me and Oliver overheard.

"I'll make it strong and sweet," I tell her as I rush toward the bar cart I set up in the living room for evenings when things are a little too much.

"How much do you hate me?" she whispers, and I barely hear her over the clinking of the glass bottles.

I turn around, holding a bottle of vodka and a bottle of the best chocolate liqueur in each hand. "Why would I hate you? Don't be silly, sissy."

She glances down, fiddling with the zipper on her jacket. "He was arrested. It's my fault."

"It's Mark's fault. Don't get it twisted in your mind, Zo. You're the victim here."

"I don't want to be a victim."

"No one does." I turn back around, figuring she needs the drink sooner rather than later. Maybe if I make it strong enough, she'll pass out on my couch and finally get some rest. Knowing my sister, she probably has barely slept since everything happened, and if she had been able to fall asleep, nightmares woke her up.

"I'm going to tell Dad everything."

I spin around so fast and without thinking, vodka goes flying in a stream across the wood floor. "Seriously?"

"He already has ideas of what happened." She shrugs as she flings herself backward into the cushion and stares up at the ceiling. "And I think he's imagining something worse. I can't leave him wondering."

"You sure about that?" I ask her. "I mean, you did nothing wrong and there's no reason to hide it from him, but don't feel like you need to because of Oliver —or me, for that matter."

She blows out a long breath. "I need to tell him for me. I didn't do anything wrong, and Dad deserves to know so his mind can stop spinning, thinking of all the worst things in the world."

"Do you want me to be there when you talk to him?" I ask her.

"No. I need to do it on my own."

I make quick work of the martini, using twice as

much of the delicious chocolate liqueur as I would if I were making the same drink at the bar. The shit is pricey, but every drop is ridiculously decadent. "If you change your mind, I'm always here for you." I turn around, walking toward her with two glasses filled to the brim. "I will always have your back."

She reaches out, wiggling her fingers as I come closer. "I made another decision too."

"What's that?" I ask as I hand her the drink, and somehow, neither one of us spills a single drop.

"One sec," she says as she lifts the martini to her lips and gulps half of it down like it's a glass of water.

I stare at her in absolute shock. Neither one of us is a big drinker, and I know that martini is hella strong, but that doesn't seem to matter to her in this moment. I take the seat next to her on the couch, staring at her over the rim of my glass as she finally pulls the drink away from her lips.

"I'm going to go to the cops about what Mark did."

My eyes widen. "You are?"

"Yeah," she says as she wipes her mouth with the back of her hand. "Or I'm going to confront him and make him drop the charges. I haven't decided which one."

"Which way are you leaning?"

"Going to him."

"Why?"

"If I go to the cops, I'll have to press charges and

testify. I don't know if I have the nerve to do that, but I know I can face him and threaten him into making this all go away for Oliver."

"I'll support you in whatever you decide, but don't feel like you need to do anything because of what's happening with Oliver. Grandpa and Oli's lawyer will handle it."

"I'd be doing it for me too."

I place my free hand on her leg, giving it a squeeze. "Whatever you want to do, I'll always have your back. But don't do it because you think I'm mad or upset. I'm not either of those about Oliver possibly going to jail," I tell her, but I'm lying. I'm upset, but not with her. I'm pissed at the fucked-up world where guys like Mark get away with assaulting women. If I had to guess, I bet this isn't the first time he's done something like this either. "I'm upset about what happened to you. Mark deserves more than one beating."

The corner of her mouth tips up as she blinks slowly, the alcohol already pressing against the right areas. "He deserves to rot in jail."

"That he does. He deserves to be someone's wife on the inside."

Her smile widens. "I like the idea of that."

"Me too," I tell her and giggle. "I can hear him screaming for help."

"Maybe I'll go to the cops instead. I'll talk to Dad about it and get his take."

"Dad will tell you to go to the cops too, Zo. You know he will. He won't want you to see Mark under any circumstances and especially not to save Oliver. You don't want to put Mark in a position of power again, and I think that's what will happen if you threaten to go to the cops if he doesn't drop the charges. You need to take the power, even if you have to testify in court. The world needs to know what he did so he doesn't do it to someone else."

"You know, I did look him up online before we started hanging out. I couldn't find anything he did besides a few traffic tickets. I thought he was safe."

I point at her with my index finger as I balance the drink in my grip. "That right there is why you should press charges. So the next woman who searches for him finds at least an arrest on his record, stopping them from becoming his next…" The end of the sentence dies on my tongue.

"Victim," she says softly. "You can say it. I know what I am even if I hate it."

"You don't have to be. You can take the power back, sissy."

She places her elbows on her legs as her shoulders slump forward. "I don't know if I can ever trust another man. How messed up is that, Lou?"

"It's why you should always pick the bear."

She nods. "I've always understood why the bear is the better choice, but they can't all be bad, can they?"

"Oliver's good," I tell her. "I'd like to believe there are more men like him than Mark."

"Dad's great, and so are all our uncles," she says, agreeing with me. "There have to be more like them out there in the world, but I don't think I have the strength to search for one anymore. I'd rather be alone."

My heart aches for my little sister. She deserves happiness just as much as the next person. I didn't want this single event to derail her chance at a happily ever after and finding the man of her dreams.

"We can be spinsters together," I tell her.

"No. You have Oliver."

"Who says he'll be around for very long?"

Zoey takes my hand in hers and stares up at me with soft eyes. "He'll be around. He's in this for the long haul, and I love him for you."

"We're so new," I tell her before taking a long sip of my drink.

"That doesn't matter. He looks at you the way Dad looks at Mom. He's over the moon for you, sis."

"A lot can happen in a short amount of time."

I don't know why I'm doubting what she's saying. I can feel things are different with Oliver than they have been with anyone else. There's an easiness to us that I've never experienced before. I feel safer with him than I have with any other man—besides those I'm related to—in my entire life.

"He's sticking around."

I set my glass down on the coffee table and relax back into the couch next to my sister. "We'll see."

"Maybe you don't see it, but I do. He'd burn the world down for you—and for me, for that matter. He already proved it, and he doesn't seem the least bit worried about going to jail for something he was doing to avenge me."

"He'd do it again too. He said it was worth it."

"See?" she says, pushing her shoulder into me. "A keeper."

"I don't know if we're even dating."

She turns her head toward me, her eyes narrowing. "What would you call it?"

"Getting to know each other."

"Lou," she breathes and shakes her head. "You don't get to know someone by doing what he did. He's in it and in it deep."

"Maybe. We haven't really talked about what we are."

"It's been busy," she says and giggles. "I shouldn't laugh."

"You laugh when you want to laugh. There's no right or wrong when you're around me."

"I love you," she says to me, resting her head on my shoulder.

"I love you too, sissy," I tell her, wishing I could take away the last few days from her memory.

"I want to find an Oliver someday."

"You will."

"Does he have a brother?" she asks and then yawns, covering her mouth with her hand.

"Yes, but he's not a good one."

"Damn," she whispers.

We sit in silence, and my sister's breathing changes, growing slower and deeper. I know she's asleep when she snores softly, something she's done since she was a little kid. I wait a few minutes before sliding out from her side and easing her onto the couch so she can get a good night's rest.

I pick up my phone from the kitchen counter and open my messages.

> Oliver: You okay?

He sent the text an hour ago. I heard the vibration from across the room, but I was too engrossed in the conversation with my sister to look.

> Me: I'm good. Zoey's here and passed out on my couch. You okay?

> Oliver: Right as rain.

> Me: Liar.

> Oliver: I'm fine. Shit'll work out.

> Me: I wish I had the faith you do in that.

> Oliver: The bad guy can't always win.

I grunt as I read his response. I've seen the bad guy win plenty of times in real life. In movies, the good guy always comes out on top, but that is a fantasy world.

Me: I hope you're right.

I glance over as Zoey shifts on the couch, and I realize she needs a blanket. My place has way too many drafts to sleep without something over you, even when the heat is on. It's the price I pay for the expansive view of the city with the floor-to-ceiling windows.

I grab a blanket from the chair across from her and cover her, pulling the material up to her chin. "Sweet dreams, sissy," I whisper as I stare down at her, knowing I'd burn the world down for her too.

Oliver: I'm heading out on a call. Catch ya later, sweetheart.

Me: I'm going to bed. Night, Oli.

Oliver: Night, beautiful.

I smile as I stare at the screen, thinking about sending him a kiss emoji back as a response. But I stop myself and send a heart instead.

Whatever this is…whatever we are becoming, I am along for the ride.

CHAPTER 12
OLIVER

"HOW DOES THIS ALL WORK?" I ask from the passenger seat of Lulu's new ride.

"They contact me on my website or social media to schedule an initial visit where I give them an estimate for the job."

I stare at Lulu's profile. "They're strangers?"

She glances at me for a second with her eyebrows furrowed. "Well, yeah."

"You don't know them at all?"

"That's what stranger means," she says as her eyes scan the highway ahead of us.

She called me this morning, asking if I wanted to take a drive up north with her to meet with a new client. I didn't have a damn thing planned and figured I'd rather spend the day in the car with her than sitting at home by myself. I'm not sure how much longer I'll have my freedom, and I don't want to waste a minute of it, especially when it comes to Lulu.

"I thought your business was word of mouth. Like people who know people you know."

She shakes her head. "No. That would be really limiting."

"But also much safer," I say to her, trying to keep the bite out of my voice.

"You worry too much."

"You worry too little." I scrub a hand down my face, wondering how she thought any of this was a good idea. "There are bad people out there, Lulu. Mark is proof of that."

"Not everyone is a Mark, Oliver."

"How do you know if they're a bad person or not before you take the appointment?"

"I don't, but I have faith in humanity."

I shake my head slowly, hating that she doesn't realize how fucking dangerous this all is. "Lulu."

"Oliver," she replies as her car tells her to turn in half a mile.

"There could be a serial killer waiting for you at this house."

"If the serial killer is named Kara who needs her pantry reorganized, then it's entirely possible."

"This isn't a joke," I tell her.

"I know. I'm not joking. I know how to protect myself, Oliver."

"So, if I'm on the other side of the door, you can protect yourself against me how exactly?"

"My dad taught me how to fight."

"I'm bigger and stronger than you are."

I can't believe we're even having this conversation. The girl is a buck fifty soaking wet, and I have easily a hundred pounds on her. She's tall for a girl, but that doesn't mean she has the muscle mass to overtake someone with my height and strength.

"I carry."

"Carry what?" I dip my gaze to her bag that looks like it's her mobile office, with a laptop, folders, and more shit than I could ever imagine carrying around.

"You know."

"You have a gun in there?" I point to the black bag that's neatly organized, but so overfull that there's no way she can easily access a weapon in a moment of terror.

"Yes."

I raise an eyebrow as I look over at her. Never in a million years would I have thought she had a gun on her. "Where is it?"

"In there."

I grunt. "No shit. I mean, where in there?"

"Under the laptop."

I drop my head and press my fingertips into my forehead in a slow rhythm, trying to stave off the headache that's right behind my skull. "You need to carry it on you or have it in a pocket that's easy for you to get to, Lou. There's no way you'll have time to move your laptop out of the way before the person strikes."

"I'll move it to a front pocket. Would that make you happy?"

"It's not about my happiness. It's about your safety."

She's barely listening to me because she's paying more attention to the navigation system than to me. This conversation isn't going the way I wanted or wished, and my words are totally falling on deaf ears.

"We're here," she says as she pulls into the driveway of a house so big, I can't even imagine the bill to heat the place in an extra-cold winter like this. "Do you think a murderer is in there?"

"Have you watched any true crime documentaries?"

"No," she says as she shuts off the engine. "I prefer rom-coms."

"Shocker," I mutter. "We're going to watch a few documentaries together."

She faces me, her eyes narrowed. "Why?"

I turn my entire body toward her, resting my back against the door. "So, you understand the reality of what's out there."

"I grew up in a Southside bar. I know all the realities. I've heard the stories. I've seen more things than I have time to explain right now, but I know. I'm not stupid, Oliver."

Well, this isn't going the way I want. "Okay," I tell her, backing off for now. I don't want to ruin the entire day, and I don't want to send her inside to meet with a new client in a shit mood. I'd hate to be the cause of her not getting a job.

"Okay?" she asks, an eyebrow raised. "We're done with this conversation?"

"Yes," I reply, but I leave out the little part about how we're not done forever, just for the moment.

"Good." She grabs her bag, hauling it into her lap. "I'll be as quick as possible, and then we can get something to eat."

"Okay, sweetheart. Take your time. I've got some shit I can do." What that shit is…I have no idea. I'll scroll on my phone or take a nap, catching up on some much-needed sleep after a long night last night.

Lulu leans over, and I meet her in the middle to give her a kiss. "I'll be careful," she says against my lips.

"I'm here if you need me," I say back, staring into her beautiful eyes.

When she pulls away and reaches for the door handle, she says, "I'll send up the bat signal if I'm in trouble." And then she's gone.

All I can do is shake my head. The girl is trouble, and her attitude is unmatched. I can't be the first person in her life who's talked to her about the dangers of going to a stranger's house. Can I? I've met her father twice now, and he seems involved and just as opinionated as she is. I've got to believe he's had a talk with her and is maybe the reason why she carries a gun, but he'd be horrified to know it's not easily accessible since she just throws it into her bag like it's a little umbrella.

I keep my eyes trained on Lulu as she saunters up the path to the front door, fixing her outfit as she walks. Damn. She's everything I always wanted in a woman but never thought I'd get. She is too good for me, but that doesn't mean I am about to quit her and whatever this is we have going on.

When the door opens, my heart slows just a little. An older woman with gray hair is standing there, and she smiles down at my Lulu with such sincerity, I can only assume she doesn't look like the serial-killer type. I slouch down in the seat, waiting for Lulu to step inside before I close my eyes.

The door to her SUV opens, and she says, "Glad to know you were ready to rescue me."

I bolt upright, my heart pounding erratically in my chest. *Fuck.* I was tired. My body isn't used to late-night shifts anymore, and my age doesn't help shit. "I knew you had it under control."

"Uh-huh," she mumbles as she slides into the seat next to me. "I survived."

"This time," I whisper as I shake the sleep from my head.

"A majority of my clients are women."

"And?" I ask, but I already know where she's going with this conversation.

"Women aren't typically murderers. It's men."

"How do you know it's going to be a woman on the other side of that door?"

"I check out their social media once they contact me, and if it's via email, I do a little research on them too. I'm very careful."

I have two choices. I could spend the day arguing with her about the holes in her client-intake process, or I could let it drop—at least for now—and have an enjoyable day with my girl.

"I know you are."

"Can we go to lunch and talk about something else?" she asks, pushing the start button to fire up the rumbly engine I love so much in an SUV like this.

"I'm down with that."

"Good. I know of a great place near here that I've been dying to try."

I don't utter the joke that clings to the tip of my tongue about how very close she actually could've been to dying by meeting a stranger at her house. *Don't be a dick, Oliver. Cut the woman some slack.*

"I'm game for whatever you are."

"Excellent," she says. "Are you a picky eater?"

I point to myself, motioning up and down my body with my fingers. "Do I look like I'm a picky eater?"

She lets out a small snort, which I find oddly adorable. "Nope."

"It's a noodle bar."

"A noodle bar?" I've never heard of such a thing. I know what a bar is, but never in my life did I think someone would or could open a noodle bar. "Do they have all types of noodles?"

"All types. It's mainly pho and ramen, but the videos I've seen make my mouth water."

"Am I going to be hungry later?" It's the only thing I hate about soups. I'm always starving within an hour or two. The liquid goes right through me. I prefer a steak and potatoes because they fill up my gut for hours and give me fuel for the entire day.

"They have other things too, Oli. I promise you won't be starving before we have a chance to make it back to the city."

"Well then, let's go to a noodle bar," I tell her, strapping my seat belt in tight because the girl isn't the best driver in the world.

I hate everyone's driving except my own, but hers is especially erratic at times. It's no wonder I met her on the side of the road with a blown tire. It's like she's scoring points for every pothole she hits because she doesn't swerve around a single one on this trip.

In less than ten minutes, we're standing inside one of the prettiest restaurants I'd ever been to in my entire life. I'm not underdressed per se, but I don't feel like my outfit of jeans and a T-shirt fits the vibe of this joint.

"Two?" a small woman asks as she grabs a few menus from a side counter.

"Yes, please," Lulu says with a bright smile. The woman radiates kindness.

"Follow me," the hostess says as she moves through the restaurant as if she's gliding.

My eyes don't know where to go first. The food on everyone's tables is both pretty and smells so good my mouth instantly waters.

The portions look large enough to fill me up, and they seem to have every variety of soup on the menu.

"Looks good, doesn't it?" Lulu asks as the woman sets menus down on either side of the table at the booth.

"I didn't realize how hungry I was until I smelled everything."

Lulu slides into the booth, and I give her a chin lift, wanting her to move over. "I want to sit next to you."

Her eyebrows rise in surprise. "Really?"

"Yeah, sweetheart. Didn't any asshole before me sit next to you?"

The hostess giggles. "Men," she whispers, shaking her head as she starts to walk away from us.

"Well, no, but my dad does that with my mom."

"Well, I do that too. I don't want to be across the

table. I want to be next to the woman I'm spending the day with."

She scoots over a few more inches, making room for me. "I like that," she says with a small smile. "But only if I get to eat off your plate."

"You can eat anything you want."

She leans over, bringing her mouth close to my ear. "Even you?"

My dick stiffens in my pants, and I growl, wishing we were anywhere except here. "Behave, Lou, or lunch is going to be much quicker than you'd like."

She pulls back and smiles at me, her cheeks pink. "I know what I want for dessert."

"What?" I ask.

"You," she says as she picks up the menu, not looking at me when she says the words.

"Eat fast," I tell her.

"No. I'm going to take my time. Good things come to those who wait."

"An idiot came up with that." I groan, shifting in my seat, hoping my cock decides to behave for the next few hours.

I scan the menu at her side, wanting to order a little of everything. Not only did I sleep like shit last night, but I barely had time to eat anything decent.

"I want to get a few apps with my noodles."

"Good plan. I want some of this too," I tell her, pointing at words I have no idea how to pronounce.

She reads where I point. "That sounds delicious."

"Everything on here does."

I'm not an uncultured guy, but some of the words are beyond my scope. I know my limits, and anything besides English has always been a struggle. I don't know why I don't bother sounding out the words, but I always figure it's better not to try than to fuck shit up.

"Do you like boba?"

"Boba like *Star Wars*?"

She turns her gaze toward me, and her eyebrows furrow as her nose wrinkles. "What?"

"Boba Fett. You know, from *Star Wars*."

"I've never watched it."

It's my turn for my eyebrows to rise. "How is that possible?"

"Girl house."

"Sad," I whisper, unable to imagine never having watched *Star Wars* in my entire life.

"We watched love stories and princesses."

"There's a princess in Star Wars."

"Does she wear a gown and a crown?"

I search my memory, flipping through the vast number of scenes. "Nope."

"Then it's a no for me."

"You wanna watch it?"

She stares at me and sighs. "Do I have to?"

"No."

"Then, no."

I chuckle.

The woman has no problem telling me what she likes and doesn't. I love the fact that she won't do something because I want her to. She sticks to her guns, and that's more than I can say about most people.

"You want to watch one of my favorite movies with me?"

"Is there a princess in it?"

"Yes."

"Does she have a sword or use a weapon?"

"No, but she has a crown and a beautiful gown."

"Is there a prince?"

"Yes, and a happily ever after."

"Does he use a sword?"

"No."

I wince. "I'd watch paint dry with you if it made you happy."

"I promise you'll like it."

The only thing I'll like is spending time with Lulu. I know the movie will be shit, but I'll trudge through it if it makes her happy and gets me closer to her.

"You want to watch it tonight?" I ask her.

"I can't. I'm doing something with Zoey later, but I'm free tomorrow."

"What are you two up to?"

"Nothing, really. Girl stuff."

That's all she needs to say for me to know I'm not invited, and I don't want to be. I have no idea what two sisters do together, but I imagine nail polish and gossip will be involved. "Another night, then."

"Another night," she says, bumping me with her shoulder as the waitress moves to our table.

"Welcome. Can I get you two something to drink?"

"I'll take a water," I say.

"Matcha."

"Got it. Be right back."

"What the hell is matcha?"

"It's a green tea that's finely ground."

"So why not just ask for green tea?"

"It's different from green tea."

"You just said it's green tea. How's green tea different from green tea?"

Lulu chuckles softly and places her hand on my arm. "You're too much sometimes."

"I know, but, Lulu…"

She turns that pretty gaze to me. "Yeah?"

"Why is shit so confusing and complicated?"

Her smile is soft and sweet. "Sometimes things are until they're right in front of you. You'll understand when you see it and taste it."

This conversation reminds me of relationships and women. They're complicated and confusing. Feelings get jumbled in a hurry. From the outside, what Lulu and I have going doesn't make sense. We're total opposites, but being on the inside, I understand how we work. We get each other, and what we don't get, we appreciate without trying to change the other person.

And when the matcha arrives, it doesn't make me understand any better.

It is green and tea but tastes like shit and doesn't remind me a damn bit of the regular green tea you get in those little paper bags to dip in hot water. It tastes like dirt, and I don't know how she can enjoy drinking it.

Her taste in everything isn't all that bad since she likes me, but I know, from this moment on, she can never pick my drinks for me for the rest of my life.

CHAPTER 13
LULU

"ARE YOU SURE ABOUT THIS?" I ask Zoey as we stand on the sidewalk outside Mark's apartment.

She peers over her shoulder at the large window in the front. "Yes, but no."

I take her hands in mine, giving them a light squeeze. "You don't need to do this."

She gives me a sad smile. "I do, though."

"No. You don't, Zo. Grandpa and Hal will figure out a way to make the charges go away without you having to talk to Mark."

"I can't take that chance, Lou. And this is about me too. I need Mark to know he doesn't hold the power here."

I can't even imagine what's going on in her head. I've never been in her situation. If I were in her shoes, would I be doing the same thing? Maybe, but I hope I never have to find out.

"If it becomes too much, just make a move, and I'm out the door with you."

"You don't need to come in with me," my sister says, always trying to be brave, even when she doesn't need to be.

"I'm going in there with you. There's no way I'd send you in there without having your back."

She throws herself against me, wrapping her arms tightly around my body. "I love you," she whispers as I hug her back, wishing I could change everything that's happened to her.

"I love you too." I glare at Mark's building, wishing we could avoid this entire confrontation.

She refused to go to the cops, preferring to handle this on her own. I tried to talk her out of it, but my sister is stubborn. She doesn't want to be dragged through the court system, having to defend herself, even though she was the victim here, not Mark. I get that. I've seen it way too many times in my short lifetime.

"I'm ready," she says as she backs away from me, letting her hands drop to her sides. "It's now or never."

I'd prefer never, but that's because I'd do anything to protect my little sister. I've spent my entire life keeping her safe, and marching into Mark's apartment feels like the most dangerous thing I've ever let her do.

We told no one we were doing this. Not our father, because he'd lose his mind. When Oliver wanted to hang out tonight, I couldn't even tell him. His response would've been even more dire than my dad's. I haven't known Oliver long, but I know him well enough to know it would be a no-go, and he'd probably tie us up to stop us from doing this.

Zoey turns around, pushing her shoulders back, walking forward with her head held high. I can feel the power radiating off her as she strides up the pathway to the building. She doesn't look like a victim. There is no meekness or fear in her long, sure strides. But I know Zoey well enough to know that she can put on a good show and that her insides are probably a shaking mess.

I stand inches behind her as she lifts her hand and knocks on his front door. I watch in amazement as she stands stiller than I've ever seen her. There is an eerie calm to her as the sound of footsteps on the other side of the door grows louder with each second.

When the door opens, a man who was probably handsome before Oliver beat his face to a pulp answers. His eyes are puffy, with dark bruises around each, spreading into his cheeks. I wince slightly, the sight of him almost overwhelming.

"Mark," Zoey says without any trace of a quaver in her voice.

He mumbles something back because his jaw is wired shut.

Damn.

Oliver really did a number on him.

But there's not an ounce of pity or sadness in me for him. He deserves everything Oliver gave him that night because of what he did to Zoey and probably other women who didn't have an Oli in their corner to beat his ass before.

She pushes Mark aside, stalking into his apartment like a boss. I follow her, doing everything I can not to brush against Mark since he never moved from the doorway.

Before I make it two steps into his place, Mark turns toward us and, with a clenched jaw, says, "What do you want?"

"To talk," Zoey says, spinning around on her heel to face Mark and me.

I stand between the two of them, knowing if something bad happens, I'll use my position to protect my little sister.

"About?" he asks.

Zoey crosses her arms, tilting her head. "You need to drop the charges."

Mark lets out an evil laugh that sends chills skittering down my spine. "No."

Zoey raises an eyebrow as she glares at him. "You know the best things about dating apps?"

He grunts.

"I was able to track down a whole bunch of women who hooked up with you before I did. Their stories are very interesting, and all of them had a very similar experience with you as I did."

Now it's my turn to widen my eyes in surprise. Zoey hasn't told me any of this. She left out important details as we drove to Mark's apartment tonight.

Mark pulls in a long breath through his flared nostrils.

"And every single one of them is ready to testify with me in open court about everything, Mark. Every dirty, despicable, degrading detail about your depravity and sexual deviances. I see a very long jail sentence in front of you."

"Bullshit," he mutters through the stiffness that looks beyond painful, even if it's deserved.

Zoey reaches into her pocket, pulling out her phone. "You want to test me?"

Mark's dark-rimmed eyes drop to the phone in my sister's hand. "You didn't find anything."

"Social media is an amazing thing, Mark. Between that and the dating app, I know everything."

"Liar," he seethes, taking a step forward, but he stops when I move in his way.

But I'm not empty-handed. I didn't bring my gun because I knew if things went badly, I might end up with the bullet or my sister would. I'm not strong enough to wrestle a man over control of a weapon.

But I did bring my strongest can of pepper spray. If he couldn't see, he couldn't attack us—or at least that was my line of thinking when I stuck it in the front pocket of my jeans.

"Does Mary Catherine ring any bells?" Zoey asks with a smug smirk on her face.

Mark's face pales beneath the bruises.

I'm not sure if I've ever been prouder of my sister than I am right now. Everything about her oozes power.

The smile on her face grows wider, and I can practically see the strength surging within her. "Want to call me a liar again?" She pauses and stares at him as his breathing grows more labored. "I want you to drop the charges against Oliver, or else me, Mary Catherine, and the handful of other women I've been able to talk to are going to the police. They may not believe one of us, but when there's a group who've all had the same fucked-up experience with you, people will listen, and you'll lose. I think there are enough of us to have your ass behind bars for many, many years."

"You wouldn't," Mark says, but his entire posture has changed. He may not be visibly shaking, but he's rattled on the inside.

Zoey lifts her chin, glaring down her nose at him. "I would, Mark. For me, there's no better fantasy than some man making you his bitch behind bars."

My knees go weak at the balls on my sister, and somehow, I don't break out in a fit of laughter at the way Mark's face contorts into something even more hideous.

"Drop the charges first thing in the morning, or we'll be at the police station tomorrow night to file charges against you. It's in your hands now," she tells him and takes a step toward the door.

But to get to the door, she needs to walk by Mark. I stiffen as she gets closer to him, hoping he doesn't try something. I let my hand drop to my pocket and to the pepper spray, ready for anything.

Zoey stops two feet in front of him. "Move," she says, motioning with the backs of her fingers like he's a fly she's shooing away.

"Zoey," he says and reaches for her.

My heart leaps in my chest and I rush forward, but Zoey takes a step back, avoiding his touch.

"Don't. Unless you want to lose that," she says with so much confidence I almost believe she could rip his hand right off without much effort.

Mark's hand drops as he steps to the side. "I'm sorry," he says, as if it's enough to make everything better.

"It's too late for that, Mark. You violated me. Your brother violated me. I'm a fool for not going to the police, but I want Oliver free and to be done with you forever. And if I hear of you doing this again, I will make sure you spend the rest of your life as someone else's bitch. Come on, Lulu."

My feet start moving as soon as hers do. Mark doesn't make a move. He stands completely still as his eyes follow our movement until he's behind us. Zoey strides out of the apartment with her head held just as high as it was when we walked in.

"You were amazing in there," I say to her. "I'm so proud of you."

She doesn't reply as she continues down the path to the driveway and then the short walk to the car. Once we're inside my SUV, she lets out a long breath. "Fuck. That was…" Suddenly, she starts to hyperventilate and pitches forward, putting her head between her knees.

I reach a hand over, rubbing her back. "You're okay," I tell her as I try to console her while she works through all the emotions that I can't fully comprehend. "You were amazing in there," I repeat because I don't think she heard me the first time.

"I was a mess," she says between rushed breaths.

"I couldn't tell, and he couldn't either. You were powerful. If I were him, I would've absolutely shat myself."

She turns her head and peers up at me, raising an eyebrow. "Shat?"

I shrug as I still my hand. "I've always liked how that word sounds."

She bursts into a fit of giggles. "You're so weird."

I'm happy my weirdness can change the mood. She can call me whatever she wants as long as she stops freaking out and her breathing returns to normal.

"Ready to go home?" I ask her as I pull my hand away from her and place it on the steering wheel.

"I could use a drink."

"You come up with the best ideas." I push the button on the dashboard, firing up the engine.

"After that, I could use a few shots of tequila to settle my nerves."

"You got it, sis," I tell her, putting my fancy SUV with so much horsepower we could get there in a few minutes if the speed limit were higher into gear. "Two tequilas coming right up."

"Three," she corrects, earning a smile from me.

A half hour later, we slide onto two stools at the bar, ready to drink away the stress.

"Well, well, well, look what the cat dragged in," Brax says as he throws a dish towel over his shoulder. "You two out looking for trouble?"

"Already did it, and now, we need to unwind," I tell him, drumming my fingernails on the wood.

"Tequila?" he asks, knowing us so damn well, but I wouldn't expect anything less since we grew up together and caused more trouble than any of us will ever fully admit to anyone outside our circle.

"Bring four shots," Zoey says before he has a chance to reach for the glasses.

His eyebrows shoot up. "Must've been a doozy."

"That's putting it mildly," I say to him as he sets four shot glasses on the bar.

"This have to do with Oliver?" Brax stares at me as he grabs the bottle of tequila and starts to pour.

"A little."

He sucks in air between his teeth. "Shit is messed up."

"What do you know about it?" Zoey asks our cousin.

"I heard someone did something to someone in our family, and Oliver took care of the guy," Brax answers.

"That all you know?" Zoey asks.

Brax nods. "It's all cryptic. I could use more specifics, but it's a need-to-know basis and I guess I don't need to know."

"It was me," Zoey admits as she wraps her fingers around one of the shot glasses. "He was protecting me."

Brax stiffens and straightens. "You could've come to me, Zo."

"Why?" she asks, slamming back the tequila as Brax and I watch her. She doesn't even wince. "So you could've been the one arrested instead?"

"Well… I…"

"Oliver was there when Zoey came to my place, Brax. We didn't keep you out of the loop on purpose, but I'm glad you're not involved."

"I've always helped," he replies.

I roll my eyes as I grab a shot glass. "Only a man would be upset that he didn't get to help and be arrested."

Brax gives me the middle finger.

"I know you always have our back, cousin," Zoey says to him, touching his hand that's resting on the bar. "I promise I didn't keep it from you on purpose."

"As long as you know I'm here." He smiles at my sister, always wanting to be the hero.

"It's not like we could forget," I tease, sticking out my tongue at him when he looks my direction.

Zoey reaches for the second shot before I'm over the burn of my first.

"Feel better?" I ask her.

"Totally." She smiles, lifting the glass to her lips.

"Do I want to know?" Brax asks, ignoring the regulars who are staring in our direction because they need refills.

"You don't," I tell him, tipping my chin toward the other end of the bar. "Looks like you have some thirsty customers."

"Fuck," he mutters, peeling away from us.

"He's nosy," I tell Zoey.

"We all are," she says and chuckles. "It's our family curse."

"Is it, though?"

She grabs a tiny red straw from the container and sticks it in her mouth. "I wouldn't have it any other way. And hey, for as much as everyone talks, Brax didn't have all the details about what happened with Oliver and Mark."

"True," I whisper. I don't know how that tidbit of information didn't work its way down the family chain.

"I'm sure Dad didn't want anyone knowing anything unless I said it was okay. It's not the kind of information you share."

"You're right," I say to her, grabbing the bottle of tequila to refill her glass. "More?"

"I think we better pace ourselves."

I giggle. "Seriously?"

"What?" she asks with a straight face.

"You've already had two. You're not pacing shit."

She moves quickly, taking the bottle from my hand. "We can switch to margaritas instead." She gets up and stalks around the bar. "Strawberry or classic?"

"Strawberry with sugar on the rim."

"You're so girlie," she says to me as she begins working her magic.

My sister has many skills, and making a margarita is one of them. We all have our specialty. That comes from growing up in a bar our family owns. I'm more of a martini girl, knowing all kinds to fit all tastes.

A minute later, she hands me a perfectly mixed strawberry margarita. "Sip slowly," she says to me like I'm the one downing alcohol like it's water.

I lift my glass as she grabs her classic on the rocks. "To girl power."

"Girl power," she says, clinking her glass with mine.

But before I can take a sip, my stomach twists.

When Oliver finds out what we did…

I place the glass against my lips, deciding to drink the worry away and deal with it all tomorrow.

CHAPTER 14
OLIVER

"DID you have fun with your sister last night?" I ask Lulu as she reaches for a container on a high shelf.

She started on organizing the garage even though I tried to talk her out of it. I love the idea in theory, but I know once she's done, I won't be able to find shit.

"Yeah. It was productive."

"Productive?"

I don't think I'd ever describe hanging out with my friends as productive. We are dumbasses and do a lot of dumbass shit, none of which is anything near productive.

My cell phone rings, drawing my attention away from her perfect ass in those damn black leggings that are my weakness. Hal's name flashes on the screen.

"Fuck," I mutter under my breath as I lift the phone, answering the call. "Hey, Hal."

Lulu glances over her shoulder with wide eyes but is quick to turn back around when I shoot her a look across the garage.

"Hey, Oliver," Hal says on speakerphone, his voice echoing through the open space. "I just got a call from the DA."

"And?"

"Something happened."

I wait for him to say more, but he doesn't.

"Okay. And?" I ask again, my leg now bouncing up and down under my desk as a sense of unease overtakes me.

"Mark is dropping the charges."

Lulu stops moving as soon as the words are out of Hal's mouth.

"He what?" I ask, figuring I heard him wrong. "Why?"

Hal blows out a breath. "Hell if I know. I'm shocked. I thought the DA was calling me to talk about a deal, but he said Mark was at his office first thing this morning and said he was withdrawing all charges against you and that it was a misunderstanding."

I blink a few times, letting everything he's said work its way around my brain. "A misunderstanding?"

"Yep. That's what he told him. Odd, right?"

"Very," I tell him, staring straight ahead.

Lulu still hasn't moved. She's like a statue, holding a box in one hand as she stands in front of the giant cabinet that's too tall even for me to reach the top without a ladder.

"So, you're in the clear. Charges have been dropped. It's the best scenario because that DA does not like to give deals to anyone, especially when there's physical violence involved."

"Thanks for your hard work, Hal."

"I didn't do much, Oliver. I didn't have a chance to. I don't know what happened with Mark, but I'm glad he had a change of heart."

"Yeah," I tell him, watching Lulu as she starts to move again, working a little faster than before. "I don't know what happened either."

"Have a good one," Hal says.

"You too, Hal," I say before disconnecting the call.

I watch Lulu, not saying a word as I set my phone back on my desk. She doesn't look at me as she continues working, searching through a container like a treasure is hidden inside.

"That's good news," she says with her back to me. "Are you relieved?"

"Yeah, but also confused." I stand, making my way across the garage until I'm right behind her.

"Why are you confused?" She doesn't bother turning around even when I know she can feel the heat radiating off my body because I'm so close behind her.

I touch her shoulders, pressing my front to her

back. "Because I don't understand why he'd drop the charges. You have any ideas?"

Her muscles are tense under my palms. "No. Not a clue." Her voice is higher pitched than normal.

Everything about the way she's acting is suspicious.

"What's productive mean, Lulu?" I graze the tender skin on the backs of her arms near her shoulders with my thumbs.

"Zoey and I…" She moans as I knead my fingers into her muscles, trying to relax the tension out of her.

"You and Zoey what?"

"We…" She leans back against me, almost melting. "You're going to be so pissed at me."

My hands still. "What did you do?"

She turns in my arms, peering up at me with her big brown eyes. "Don't be mad, okay?"

My teeth grind together as I gaze down at the woman I'm quickly falling for. She has a big heart. Her brain sometimes short-circuits, but everything else about her is more than I could ever dream. "I can't promise anything, but I need to know. What did you and Zoey do, Lulu?"

She gives me a smile that quickly fades. "We *may* have gone to Mark's place."

My entire body stiffens, and my stomach twists like someone stuck a dagger in me and scrambled everything up. "You what?" I take a step back, feeling a fire flicker to life inside me. "You went to his place?"

Lulu clasps her hands together in front of herself and twists her upper body back and forth like a little kid does when they've been busted doing something they know they shouldn't have done. "Zoey wanted to talk to him."

I rub my forehead, digging my fingertips into my skin. "Of all the shit…"

Lulu steps closer, barely leaving any space between us. "We were safe."

I close my eyes, trying to remember she is safe. She's here with me, and Mark didn't do something to Zoey or her. "Is that what productive meant?"

She nods slowly. "Zoey told him to drop the charges, or she was going to the police to file an assault charge against him."

"Fuck," I groan, hating that she faced that piece of shit. "You two should've let me handle him."

"We did that once," she says, as if somehow their stupid idea was the best solution. "And Mark listened. You're not in trouble anymore."

"There's always a price, Lulu. You think Mark's just going to forget about everything?"

She wraps her arms around my middle, placing her head on my chest. "You're mad, aren't you?"

"Mad? No," I tell her, placing my arms around her shoulders, holding on to her tightly as I bury my face in her hair. "I'm fucking terrified."

"Don't be. It's all good."

"It's not that simple for guys like him. I can't believe you went there. You could've been hurt."

"I had protection."

"Please tell me you didn't bring your gun."

"No. Of course not. I brought pepper spray."

I groan.

"We were safe. It's hard to hurt someone when you can't breathe or see."

"It's hard to run when you can't either. Pepper spray in a small space affects more than just the target."

"Oh," she whispers like she hadn't thought about that fact before now. "Then it's a good thing I didn't have to use it."

"Look at me."

She doesn't move.

"Lulu, look at me," I plead with her.

She releases her hold on me just enough to stare up at me. "Yeah?"

"Promise me you'll never do anything like that again."

"Well…"

"Promise."

"I promise," she says with absolutely no conviction to her voice.

"I mean it."

"Me too," she says.

I study her gaze, hoping she isn't lying. "I

would've burned the world down if something had happened to either of you."

"We're okay."

"Don't you ever put yourself in harm's way for me. Do you understand?"

She narrows her eyes as she stares up at me. "But it's okay if you do?"

I lift my hand, palming her cheek. "I will always protect you."

"This is a two-way street, Oliver."

"It's not," I tell her firmly as I stroke her cheek with my thumb.

A low grumble escapes her lips. "I would never let you sacrifice yourself at my expense."

"It's not your call to make, sweetheart."

"Why?" she asks, her face scrunched up in the cutest expression.

"Because you're mine," I tell her, stepping over the edge of casually dating to something serious.

Her eyes soften as her mouth opens then quickly snaps shut again.

Before she has a chance to say anything—and by anything, I mean argue with me—I lean forward and cover her mouth with mine. The kiss isn't soft and gentle. It's not sweet or innocent. This is a moment where my lips demand her obedience and submission, wanting her to know she's mine, and in return, I'm hers.

Lulu melts into me, becoming putty in my hands

as she finds the hem of my T-shirt with her fingers and slides them beneath. The coolness of her touch makes the skin on my back pebble under her caress.

My hand slips to the back of her neck, holding her closer, bending her to give me more access. I deepen the kiss, our tongues tangling together like it's a battle neither one of us wants to lose.

The shop is closed, and tonight, Liam's busy taking Sharla out of town to some convention. The garage isn't a place people wander into unless they're meant to be here or have an appointment.

When Lulu arrived, I locked everything up, making sure we wouldn't have any interruptions. I had plans for tonight, none of which included finding out I wouldn't be facing jail time, but all of them ended with Lulu naked and underneath me.

She digs her fingernails into the skin at my sides. "I need you inside me."

Her words crash over me like a wave, causing my control to slip from the final tether that had held it in place.

"Mine," I growl, wishing life could always be like this.

Lulu slides her fingers down, the nails scraping against my skin hard enough they'll leave a mark. My hand finds her ass, hauling her upward with one arm. As if she's done it a thousand times before, she spreads her legs and latches them around my middle, but our mouths never leave each other.

I carry her to my desk, setting her down in front, and finally break the kiss. "Strip," I tell her as her eyes blaze bright.

Without an argument, she moves quickly, tearing off her top, taking the bra with it. I'm not even sure the fabric hits the floor before her hands are at the waistband of her pants. Leggings are great for looking, but when it comes to quick access and getting them off, they're the absolute worst.

Her leggings are finally down, and she kicks them off, nearly panting under the weight of my gaze. My hands find the button on my jeans, working faster than they ever have before. In under thirty seconds, we're both naked and panting.

There's nothing that needs to be said. We both know what we want. What we need.

Our mouths come together again as she nearly hurls herself against me. We're a tangle of limbs and tongues, moaning as our hands roam each other's naked bodies.

Lulu places a hand against my chest, pushing me downward, and I let my body crumple to the floor.

"Lie back," she whispers against my lips. "I want to ride you."

I do as I'm told because nothing in this moment sounds better. Being inside Lulu is like tasting a piece of heaven and having her above me where I can see and touch her, watching her fall apart, is nothing short of nirvana.

My head is barely against the rug under my desk when she lines her body up and spears herself on my cock. I'm momentarily winded by the sheer amount of pleasure that spreads throughout my body. I find her hips with my hands as she rises, about to slam back down to me.

I try to slow her movement, but there's no stopping her. She has a look in her eyes that tells me there isn't a thing in the world that could control her in this moment, especially me.

I can't take my eyes off her as her hair sways and her hips move, riding me like she is racing toward the finish line. Her fingers curl into my pecs, her nails nearly piercing the skin.

When she moans, I nearly come undone underneath her. I can feel the orgasm clawing up my insides. I try to push it down, but I know I'm fighting a losing battle. With the way she's fucking me, I can't stop the freight train that's barreling toward me.

I let her take what she wants, hurtling right off the cliff. My eyes snap shut as the wave crashes over, stealing my breath and my very ability to think. Before the pleasure ebbs, Lulu follows me over, moaning my name as her movements slow until she finally collapses forward on top of me.

"Damn," she gasps, breathing heavily and trying to regain her equilibrium.

I trail a line down her spine with my fingertips. "Yeah," I mutter as I wait for my heart to slow.

She lifts her head, her eyes finding mine. "I need more," she whispers, "but I understand if you need time to recover. Age and all..."

She's fucking with me. I know. She's challenging me, and because I'm a man who never backs down, I roll over until I'm on top of her. "My girl gets whatever my girl wants," I tell her, letting the remark about my age slide. I crawl backward, spreading her legs until I'm nestled in between. "I'm not stopping until you beg me."

"Oh," she says, looking down her body at me. "I like this challenge."

"Me too," I say as my mouth finds her flesh, and it takes three orgasms until she finally begs me to stop, but I make her have a fourth before I relent.

CHAPTER 15
LULU

"ARE YOU READY FOR THIS?"

Oliver looks at me and then back to the exterior façade of the Hook & Hustle. "I don't know."

He's adorable when he's like this. He's always so sure of himself with his cocky grin and pushed-back shoulders, looking larger than life.

I take his hands in mine and smile. "They already love you."

His forehead crinkles in just the right way to make him look more distinguished. "Why?"

"Because you're a protector."

"You mean I have a record."

I shake my head, keeping my eyes on his. "My family doesn't care about that. Hell, my grandpa has a record too, but his crime wasn't noble like yours. And you don't have a record, Oli. It was wiped away."

"Don't get me started," he grumbles, still salty over our field trip to Mark's apartment. It's going to take time for him to get over it.

"You've met almost everybody anyway," I tell him, ignoring the sour look on his face. "There are only a few more."

"But all at once." He draws in a deep breath and cracks his neck. Ouch. I don't understand how people can do that without using their hands, and even if they can, why the hell they'd do it in the first place.

"Come on." I pull him toward the door because my stomach is rumbling, and it's not warm enough to stand outside much longer to have a conversation.

When the door opens and we step inside, everyone turns their attention our way.

"Fuck," Oliver whispers.

"Hey," I call out, giving a one-handed, half-assed wave to my entire family.

But in true Gallo fashion, a second later, they go back to their conversations and ignore us.

"See," I tell Oliver, pitching my thumb toward the dining room where everyone is milling around. "They don't care."

"Sure," he says, his front plastered to my back. "They're luring me in and making me feel safe."

I swat at him over my shoulder. "Don't be ridiculous."

Zoey waves her hand, drawing our attention. We

move through the dining room, stepping around clusters of other cousins in conversation to get to Zoey's table.

"Hey there. Welcome," Zoey says to Oliver. "Want a beer or something?"

"Sure," he says, but there's a quaver to his voice.

"We won't judge if you drink a beer, Oliver. We own a bar, for shit's sake," Zoey tells him. "You want something stronger to get through this night?"

Oliver's shoulders finally relax. "Just a beer, Zo."

"You want to have a margarita with me?" I ask my sister, hoping she'll make them too.

"You got it, sis," she says before she gets up from the table and stalks toward the back of the bar.

"Going for the hard stuff tonight?" he asks me as he sits down in an empty seat, and I take the one next to him.

"Are you judging me?"

He shakes his head. "Nope. Just wondering if you weren't entirely truthful about how the night will go."

"It'll be fine," I tell him. "I just like the taste of a margarita, and Zoey makes the best ones in the world."

He studies my face, and for a moment, I don't think he believes me. "We'll see who's right."

I roll my eyes, wishing he'd understand my family is the least judgmental group of people he's probably ever met in his entire life.

"It's good to see you again," my uncle Vinnie says,

holding out his hand to Oliver as soon as he's close enough.

"You too," Oliver says, shaking my uncle's hand while maintaining eye contact with him.

"I'm Vinnie. The uncle."

Oliver gapes as who Vinnie is—or, I should say, was—finally hits him. "Wait a minute."

Vinnie's hand stops moving, but he doesn't let go of Oliver's. "Yeah."

"You played football."

"Yep. A few years."

"You were my favorite player growing up."

That's so sweet. My uncle Vinnie loves to hear from fans, even after all these years. The man adores anything that fuels his ridiculously large ego.

"Shit, I'm a dinosaur. I know that's supposed to make me feel better, but now I feel ancient."

"I meant when I was a teenager. You made me want to shoot for playing football professionally. I thought I could do it."

"And did you?"

I watch the two of them bonding over sports. I hate anything that makes me sweat, and therefore, all athletic things are off the table for me. The moment is sweet.

"No. I went into the service instead."

"Honorable," my uncle says, giving Oliver a genuine smile.

"I watched every game of yours besides the few

that happened while I was at boot camp. No television there."

"Really?" Vinnie asks.

Oliver nods. "There wasn't shit. No TV. No newspaper. No phone. No internet. No communication with the outside at all. The world could've ended, and I wouldn't have known the difference."

"I could never," Vinnie says softly, shaking his head. "I'm too addicted to my phone."

"You don't say," I tease my uncle. The man is on it a lot, checking his social media and my aunt Bianca's.

"Zip it," he says to me with a smirk on his face. "You kids aren't any better."

I love that he still calls us all kids, even though we're fully grown and Tate has her own. I don't think the older generation will see any of us as adults for a very long time. We'll have to have gray hair and a smattering of wrinkles before they realize we're grown up, but I'm not sure even that'll be enough.

"Everything okay from the other day?" Vinnie asks Oliver.

Oliver grunts as he slices his eyes to me. "Zoey and Lulu took matters into their own hands."

Vinnie's gaze snaps in my direction, and I wish I could scurry under the table and hide.

"Tattletale," I mutter to Oliver.

"What did you two do?" Vinnie asks.

"What are we talking about?" Zoey asks, oblivious

to the conversation as she sets down two margaritas and Oliver's beer.

"Your field trip," Oliver says to her.

Zoey freezes before she has a chance to take a sip. "Um, what field trip?" she asks, pretending not to know anything.

I pull the margarita in front of me as my stomach rumbles but, this time, not from hunger. "We didn't do anything any man in this family wouldn't do if they were in our shoes," I say with confidence because every word is the truth.

Men do whatever they want. They don't ask for permission, and they sure as hell don't worry about the consequences, especially when someone they love is in danger.

"Tell me I'm wrong," I say, challenging my uncle and Oliver.

"Well, no," Vinnie says, placing his hand on the back of my chair. "You're not wrong, kiddo. But we have the strength when something goes wrong because it usually does."

"She had pepper spray," Oliver says.

I reach over and smack his arm. "Whose side are you on?"

"The side of you staying alive."

I grunt, and my eyes go wide as I spot my dad walking our way.

"What's going on?" Dad asks as his gaze moves around the table before landing on his brother.

"We're talking about a field trip," Vinnie tells him, ratting us out.

What is it with the men in my life not being able to keep their big mouths shut? It's so annoying.

"What field trip?" Dad asks through gritted teeth and a clenched jaw, but this time, he's staring only at me and Zoey, who's next to me.

"The charges were dropped against Oliver," Zoey says without answering his question and incriminating us in something we don't need to be lectured about like we're teenagers again.

"What are we talking about?" Mom asks as she comes next to Dad, sliding her arm into the crook of his to lock them together. "I've seen that look before, and it doesn't mean anything good."

"Your daughters took a field trip," he says to her.

"This is my moment to dip," Uncle Vinnie says, giving me a wink before he peels away from the table, leaving us with a mess to deal with.

Jerk.

"Did you go to the Mag Mile?" Mom asks, and I love her for not thinking anything bad immediately, unlike my father.

"Sweetheart," Dad whispers as he pats her hand softly where it rests on his forearm. "I don't think it was that type of field trip."

"Oh." Mom's eyebrows rise. "Let's sit."

Shit.

"It's not a big deal," I say, trying to alleviate the tension that's starting to bubble around us.

Mom and Dad sit across from Zoey and me, looking at us with an expression I saw one too many times as a teenager. "Talk," Dad says in that voice that always made my asshole pucker a little bit as a kid.

"It was my idea," Zoey says with her chin held high, looking like the badass little sister I always knew she was. "I wanted to take the power back."

"Shit," Mom mutters.

"And what does that mean?" Dad asks, wanting more details because he can never move on without a full explanation. He should've been a detective because he would've solved every case with his inability to let shit go.

"Do not tell me you talked to Mark," Dad adds.

"Talk?" Oliver barks out a bitter laugh.

Dad's look only hardens.

"I couldn't let Oliver go to jail," Zoey explains. "Mark doesn't get to have that power."

"Go on," Mom says in a voice that is soft like she totally understands and is going to be on our side when we finally give them all the details.

"We went to his place a few nights ago, and Zoey talked to him."

If I thought my dad's body posture was stiff before, I was wrong. His back is ramrod straight, and I'm not even sure he's breathing because he's so still. "You fucking did what?"

Oh boy.

When he throws out the curse word so casually, we know we are in trouble.

Zoey glances at me and I cringe, but I'm happy she's in the middle of the shitstorm with me.

"Dad, we're grown, and if Zoey wanted to confront him, I was going to have her back. I went with her to make sure she was safe."

Dad's gaze slides to me, and he doesn't look the least bit at ease by my statement. "You should've called me or tried to talk her out of it."

"As a fully grown adult, I'm able to make my own decisions without my sister having to call my father to stop me. I'm not an idiot. I knew it was dangerous, but I couldn't sleep at night and live with myself if Oliver went to jail over something Mark did to me. To *me*, Dad. Not you. Not her. Not Mom. To me. I hated feeling out of control and helpless. I took it back. I went there and threatened him. I had evidence to back me up, and Mark knew I had his balls and life in my hands. He backed down and dropped the charges yesterday."

"Jesus," Mom whispers, covering her mouth with her hand. "You two could've been hurt. The man isn't stable."

"I brought my pepper spray," I add, thinking Dad would be happy to hear I, at least, brought something to protect us.

Dad closes his eyes, swearing under his breath.

That isn't the reaction I thought I'd get from him, so I go on, trying to make him feel better.

"It's over. Zoey got through to him, and we left without an issue. We're safe. We're here."

Dad's eyes snap open, and there's a fire I'm not sure I've ever seen burning inside them. "It's over?"

I nod, and so does Zoey.

"It's never over with guys like him."

"That's what I said," Oliver adds, earning himself a glare from me. "You don't know guys like him, Lulu."

"You girls could've been really hurt," Mom says, filled with concern instead of burning anger like our dad.

"But we weren't," Zoey tells her as she grabs her margarita and takes the biggest sip. She's going to feel that working through her system quickly, which is probably a good thing.

"I think you should come stay with us for a little while," Dad says to Zoey.

Zoey's eyebrows rise over the salted rim. "Uh, no. That's a hard pass."

"It's not safe for you to be home alone."

"I have a gun," she says plainly, as if she's talking about a new pair of shoes and not a deadly weapon.

Dad tips his head back, staring up at the ceiling, and lets out another extremely long and detailed string of curse words.

"Maybe just for a few days," Mom says, holding on to Dad's hand so hard her knuckles are white.

"She can stay with me. Good?" I ask them, knowing they're right. Zoey needs to stay somewhere until we know Mark won't retaliate, but staying in her childhood bedroom isn't the answer.

"I'll stay with Lulu," Zoey says, dipping her head in my direction because she's happy I opened my mouth to give her another option.

"Dinner," Grandma announces at the perfect moment.

Saved by food.

"I don't regret what I did, Dad. Oliver doesn't have to go before a judge for something he should've never been involved with, and I don't feel like a complete victim the way I did before. I took that power back, and I'll never feel sorry about that."

"Come on, sweetheart. Let it go for now," Mom says. "The girls are safe, and you taught them to stick up for themselves. They did that. They've been through enough and don't need you losing your shit about it now."

"I want them to come to me," he explains to her.

"I know, baby. You protected them their entire lives, but now they're adults. Lulu has Oliver, and Zoey does too, in a way. You taught them to be strong, independent women. Look at them. They're everything we could've wished for."

Dad's gaze moves in our direction, and his face

softens. "You're right, Delilah. Our girls are strong and brave, but that also scares the absolute shit out of me. If something were to happen to either of you…" he says, his voice cracking on the last word as he shakes his head, unable to finish the statement.

"I'll watch over them," Oliver promises my father.

Mom touches Dad's cheek, trying to console him. I'm not sure I've ever seen him in such a state in my entire life. "They're good, Lucio."

Dad lets out a shaky breath. "You're right."

"I know," Mom says with a sweet smile. "But I usually am."

"Thank you," Dad says to Oliver. "I'm glad they have someone else they trust to have their backs."

"Always," Oliver says to my dad with a dip of his head.

"I love you two more than the air I breathe. Don't do any more boneheaded shit, okay?"

I nod, and Zoey says, "We promise."

"Love you two," Mom says, pulling Dad up from the table. "The lasagna is going to be cold if you wait much longer."

"It's as hot as lava for an hour," Dad tells her as he straightens and takes a step toward the bar, where all the food has been put out by my aunts.

"Fuck. That was intense," I say when they're far enough away not to overhear us. "And you—" I turn to Oliver and pin him with a glare "—have a big mouth."

He shrugs, taking a pull of his beer so he can't defend himself—although he probably doesn't want to argue with me in front of my entire family.

"He took that pretty well," Zoey says about our dad.

"No. He didn't," I refute, shaking my head.

"Better than I thought," she adds.

"He definitely could've been worse." I sigh and lift my margarita to my lips. "I'm glad I went for something stronger today."

"I may need a second," Zoey says with a giggle as she downs half of what is left in her glass, and I watch in amazement at how easily she's drinking it.

"We'll make drinks tonight at home," I tell her. "We'll swing by your place and grab your things first, and then it's movies and margaritas."

"Can I come?" Oliver asks.

"No," I tell him, wanting a night alone with my sister. "People with big mouths don't get to enjoy movies and margaritas with us."

Oliver grunts as he slides his arm around the back of my chair, touching my shoulder. "Baby," he whispers in my ear, causing my skin to pebble at the deepness. "You sure liked my big mouth this morning when it was—"

"Okay," I say, shooting up out of my chair and trying to keep my face from flushing any more than it already is. "We better grab our plates."

Zoey giggles as she pushes herself up from the

table. "I love you two together. You can totally come to movie and margarita night, Oli."

Oliver smiles over at my sister as I mouth, "Traitor."

"What are we watching?" he asks her.

"*Pretty Woman*," she answers.

"Fuck," he says.

The regret on his face is instant. Serves him right.

CHAPTER 16
OLIVER

"WHEN DO I get to meet her?" Mom asks as she pours herself a fresh cup of coffee in the middle of the afternoon.

"Whenever you want, Mom."

"Randall said she's lovely."

"Were those his words?" I raise an eyebrow.

In my entire life, I've never heard Randall call anyone lovely. He isn't a mean guy, but his vernacular isn't that proper.

"He said she was pretty and kind. He said he liked her for you."

"That's different from lovely, but all of it is true. Although, I think she's too good for me."

Mom waves me off. "No one is too good for my boy," she says, reaching across the table to pinch my cheeks like she's done since I was a little boy.

"Ma," I say, rubbing the skin she just assaulted as soon as she lets go. "Stop that shit."

She laughs as her hands move to her coffee mug, which is far safer for my face. "Is she the one, baby?"

I stare at my mother, turning over how I want to answer the question. The simple answer is yes. In a short amount of time, Lulu Gallo has stolen my heart. It's never happened for me before. Not like this. Not this fast. Everything with her has come easy, including the feelings. But I know my mom. If I answer yes, she'll start planning the wedding before I even have a chance to ask Lulu the big question.

"I'll take that as a yes," she says before I mutter a reply. "I need to meet her as soon as possible if she's going to be my daughter-in-law."

"No."

"No?" Ma's eyebrows rise. "Why?"

"Because Lulu doesn't know she's going to be your daughter-in-law yet, and I don't want you to scare her off."

"Baby," she says with a sweet smile, "would I do that?"

"Yes."

"I can keep my lips closed."

I stare at her because we both know that's a lie.

"I *can* do it if it's necessary. I don't *like* to do it, but I can, Oli."

"I'll think about it."

Mom rolls her eyes as she lifts the coffee to her lips

and blows across the top. "Invite her over for dinner this weekend. For me. Please," she begs, knowing I find it hard to say no to her anytime, let alone when she gives me those puppy-dog eyes.

"Fine. Fine. I'll ask her if she's free."

"She can pick the night."

Damn. She's trying everything in her arsenal to make sure she meets Lulu sooner rather than later. "I will."

"Hey. Hey. I'm here," Liam announces as he walks through the front door. I groan as he kicks off his shoes. "Sharla wasn't feeling well, so I came alone."

"Good," Ma says, "Not about Sharla, but that you're here. There's something I want to talk to both of you about."

"What's wrong?" I ask her, ignoring my brother as he stalks into the kitchen and pours himself a cup of coffee too.

"We'll wait for your brother."

I point at him.

"Fine," she says with a sigh. "Randall and I are working on our wills."

My stomach turns. I hate talking about death. It's like I'm mentally allergic to the topic and have been since I was a little kid.

"You're too young for that shit," Liam says to her as he sets down his black coffee on the table and takes a seat.

"Baby," she turns toward him and smiles, "I'm not young. I don't know how many years I have left on this planet—"

"No one does," I tell her. "But why now?"

"I had a little health scare," she says, like she's talking about the weather and not something more serious. "But everything's fine."

"What the hell, Ma?" Liam says with wide eyes. "Why didn't you say anything?"

"I didn't want you two to worry."

She's been that way her entire life. The only things she's good at keeping secrets about are herself and her health. The woman is a nosy open book otherwise, but as soon as it involves her well-being, she's tight-lipped.

"I'd rather know than be blindsided," I tell her.

"If the tests would've come back with something bad, I would've told you then, but there was no need for all of us to worry until I knew for sure."

"So, you worried alone?" I ask.

"No. I had Randall."

Liam grunts. "He's about as sincere as an alley cat, Ma."

"Oh, stop." She swats Liam's arm. "You know Randall loves me and worships the ground I walk on. I couldn't have asked for anything more from him while we waited for the tests to come back."

Randall isn't a bad dude. He's obsessed with money, but so many people are these days. He's everything you'd think of when picturing a car salesman. Everything is about the deal unless it has to do with my mother. He's always been sweet to her, something our biological father didn't seem capable of doing.

"Anyway," she says, reaching over to the counter and grabbing a stack of papers, "we're finalizing our wills—I mean trusts. I keep getting that wrong. Trusts are for fancy people, and Randall says we need them."

"Don't know the difference. Don't care either," Liam says before he takes a sip of the awful coffee. My mother likes her coffee strong and bitter and has since I was a little kid.

"It means when we die, you won't have to go to court to inherit everything. And if either of us becomes seriously ill, you won't lose everything we spent a lifetime building to a care facility."

The very thought of my mother getting older and being put in a place like that makes my blood boil. "I'll take care of you if you get too sick," I tell her, knowing I'll do anything for the woman who gave me life.

"You're sweet, baby," she says.

"You're always nicer to him," Liam complains with a sour look.

"He's always nicer to me," she replies.

Liam shakes his head and glares at me. "Suck-up."

I give him the middle finger.

"It's like sitting here when you two were teenagers," she says.

My phone vibrates, and I glance down, seeing a message from Lulu.

> Lulu: Headed out to an appointment. I'll text you when I'm on my way back to the city.

> Me: Send me your location.

> Lulu: Why?

> Me: Safety, babe.

I swear I can hear Lulu groan from here. But there's something about her job that has me on edge. It would be different if she had an assistant with her, but going alone to stranger's houses isn't something I'm comfortable with. She knows how I feel, but she's not having it.

"What's wrong?" Mom asks.

I glance up and meet my mother's eyes. "Lulu's going to work."

"Okay, but what's with the face? You look worried."

I scrub a hand across my beard and exhale, trying to work out the tension that's now perpetually in my shoulders. "I hate her job."

"What's she do?"

"She's an organizer."

Mom tilts her head like she didn't hear a word I said. "A what?"

"She's a home organizer. She goes to clients' homes and organizes all their shit."

"Does she know these people?" Mom asks.

"Nope."

Liam sucks in a breath between his teeth. "I'd never let Sharla do that shit."

I don't want to argue with him over Sharla. He's perfectly fine with her taking off her clothes for a bunch of sex-depraved men every night, which is ridiculous, but then again, he's one of those guys watching her.

"That's dangerous," Mom replies.

"Exactly," I tell her.

"Are they vetted in any way?"

I shake my head.

Mom's lips twist. "How does she find new customers?"

"Mainly social media."

Mom sits back and shakes her head. "That girl has a death wish, baby. You better set her ass straight."

"I just told her to share her location with me so I at least know where she is if something ever goes wrong."

"If you're going to marry this girl, you're going to need to lay down the law."

Liam's eyes snap to me. "Marriage?"

"Mom."

"Sorry," she says with a grimace.

"You're going to marry her?"

"Someday," I tell him.

"Good."

"Good?" I ask my brother, wondering when this nicer side of him happened.

"She's good for you. I like her."

"You like her?" I ask, raising an eyebrow.

He nods. "You're less grumpy with her around."

"Whatever," I mumble.

"Well, at least most of the time," he adds and laughs.

"I have a bad feeling I can't quite shake," I tell my mother.

"About Lulu?" she asks.

"About her work. Every day, I wake up with a pit in my stomach when I know she's going to meet a new client."

"Maybe you need to become her assistant," Liam tells me. "I can handle the garage."

"That'll go over like a ton of bricks, and I know nothing about organizing. I don't think she'd go for it or believe my intentions were more for the business than her protection. And then there's the fact that I'd rather stick a hot poker in my eye than organize someone else's mess."

"Couldn't agree more," Liam says with a tip of his head.

It's the only way we're able to work together without being at each other's throats all the time. If one of us were organized and the other weren't, we'd be in constant battle with as much shit as we have at the garage. My mother had her hands full trying to get us to clean our rooms when we were young. In the end, we usually jammed all the shit into our closets and closed the door, pretending that we'd done something productive.

"Well, I hope for her sake, our worry is for nothing," Mom says as she places her hand over mine. "But maybe have the conversation with her."

"I have."

"Do it again. Sometimes it takes a few times for the words to actually stick."

"I'll try."

"Okay. Now, back to the trust."

I grumble under my breath, hating everything about the conversation today. No one's ready to talk about their parents' mortality, even though we're all going to face it someday.

"Oliver, you're going to be executor."

"What the hell?" Liam asks, lifting his arms wide. "Why not me?"

"Baby, you're still going to get half of everything, but Oliver will have to do all the paperwork. Would you rather have to do the paperwork?"

My brother drops his arms back down. "No."

Mom's smooth. She knew exactly what to say to calm my brother down. "I didn't think so," she says.

"Randall and I are leaving everything to you two, and there's a lot. Between the house, the cars, the accounts, it's well over a couple million dollars in assets."

Liam nearly swallows his tongue at that figure. As soon as he has money in his hands, he spends it. He's never had more than a few thousand in an account and probably never will, especially with Sharla around.

"I'd rather have you than the money, Ma," I say to her.

"Me too," Liam says, and there's sincerity in his voice, which shocks me.

"Randall thinks of you two as his boys, and since he's not close with anyone else in his family and I'm not close with anyone else in mine, it'll all go to you two."

"Thanks, Ma," Liam says.

She pins him with a stare. "Do not spend it all on ass and tits either. We worked too hard for that money for it to go into some woman's G-string."

I burst into laughter. She knows her son. There's no denying what kind of human he is since she breathed life into him.

"Damn, Ma."

"Don't damn, Ma me. I know what you do. Boy

has been led around by his dick since the moment he realized he had one."

"I won't spend it on tits and ass," he grumbles. "I'll save it."

"Liar," she mutters and shakes her head. "Buy yourself a house or something."

"I plan to do that way before you die."

"I like to hear that. I'd like to be a grandmother before I go. Can one of you make that happen?" She shifts her stare between the two of us, waiting for a response.

"I'm not ready to be a dad," Liam tells her, speaking the truth. The man is barely a grown-up most days, and there's no way he could be responsible for a tiny human when he's barely responsible for himself.

"I have to marry the girl before we have a baby," I say to her.

"No, you don't."

"I do, Ma." I shake my head. "I want to enjoy my wife a little while before we start a family."

"Well, put a ring on it quick and get to *enjoying* her. That's how babies are made."

"You don't say," I tease her, smiling at her as my phone rings. I glance down, and it's the business line. "I've got to go."

Liam's eyes dip to my phone. "Want me to grab it?"

I shake my head. "I don't have shit to do for a

while. I got this one," I tell him as I stand up, putting the phone to my ear. "Hello."

"Bye, baby," Mom whispers, pulling me down by my arm to kiss my cheek.

"Bye, Mom," I mouth back. "How can I help you?" The lady on the other end explains her problem and location as I make my way outside to my truck. "I'll be there in twenty."

The afternoon is busier than I expected. With the sun shining most of the day, I didn't think there'd be many people who needed a tow. Boy, was I wrong. The potholes on the city streets have become so bad, people's tires are getting fucked up quicker than I can tow them in. Bad for them, but great for the business.

I hadn't even noticed that it was after five, and I haven't heard from Lulu in hours. As soon as I climb out of the truck and transfer the business line to Liam's cell, I shoot Lulu a text.

> Me: Just checking in and getting an
> ETA for dinner tonight.

I wait, staring at the phone, but the three little dots don't appear and the message stays unread.

Liam's sitting at his desk, ready for the evening shift, picking up right where I left off.

"What happened?" he asks as soon as I make it to my desk and collapse back into the seat.

"Busy day, and Lulu hasn't messaged in a while."

"When did you hear from her last?"

I scroll back and realize she hasn't messaged since she arrived at her client's house, which was hours ago. "Fuck," I growl, swiping my finger over the location button. She hasn't moved either. She's still an hour outside the city in a northern suburb that's filled with expensive homes and old money.

"What?" Liam asks, his eyes fixed on me.

"She hasn't moved."

"I'm sure she's busy in someone else's junk drawer."

Maybe the location isn't updating because she's in an area without cell service. It happens to me all the time on the road. I press the location button again, hoping it'll show she moved. "Damn it," I mutter as my heart starts to pick up pace.

"You're really worried."

"Duh," I tell him as I try to convince myself everything is fine. I don't want to overreact, causing Lulu to get pissed at me and ruining the entire night we have planned.

"Call her sister. Maybe she's heard from her."

I swipe over to a new message and shoot one off to Zoey. She entered her number into my phone the other night when she agreed to stay at Lulu's place for a few days. She said it was for her safety, but now I know it was for my sanity.

> Me: Zoey. It's Oliver. Have you heard from Lulu since she left?

It only takes a minute before the three little dots start moving.

> Zoey: No. I usually do, but not today. Weird.

I shoot up from my chair as a knot forms in my stomach.

"Where are you going?" Liam asks as I grab my keys off my desk.

"To wherever her phone is to find my girl."

"Oh boy. Be safe," he says as I open the top drawer of my desk and grab a small Glock I keep in there just in case, even if I thought I'd never need it. "Call me if you need bail money."

"Have it ready, because if something's happened to her, someone's going to take their last breath," I tell him as I stalk out of the garage, ready to find my girl and make sure she's all right.

CHAPTER 17
LULU

I TAKE a last sip of my iced coffee, ready to get this final appointment of the day started. Oliver and I have plans later, and I can't wait to try a new restaurant that opened down the street.

I shoot off a text to Oliver, letting him know I arrived and will be unavailable for a while. He's been worried lately and reminds me more of a paranoid father than a boyfriend.

> Me: Headed out to an appointment.
> I'll text you when I'm on my way back
> to the city.

Only a few seconds pass before he replies.

> Oliver: Send me your location.

I groan as I stare at the screen, my eyes stuck on his words.

Me: Why?

Oliver: Safety, babe.

I'm not dumb enough to think I'm invincible. I know the realities of walking into strangers' houses and being a woman in today's society. It's almost impossible to trust anyone anymore.

Even though I hate the idea, I turn on my location sharing with Oliver so he'll have peace of mind. I already share my location with my sister and parents, something they required when I was younger and never stopped because I didn't feel like there was a need to.

Me: Done. Talk soon.

I tuck my phone into my bag and climb out of my car, soaking in the warm sunshine and the crisp air. Spring is near. I can feel it. Only a few more weeks before the frigid temperatures completely vanish until next year. It can't come soon enough. This winter has been brutal.

The house is beautiful and looks like it could be in an architectural magazine, but that's not uncommon for homes in this area. One thing I love about my work is seeing the insides of houses that I would never be able to see otherwise. Even the most put-together houses when it comes to decorating have overfilled closets and too many junk drawers stuffed with items the homeowner will never use.

I knock on the door and glance down at my watch. I'm right on time. I need to cut down on the small talk and get to work so I can be home at a decent hour and miss the worst part of rush-hour traffic. It doesn't matter if you're going into the city in the afternoon, it'll still be awful.

The door opens, and I glance up, my eyes locking on someone I never thought I'd see again. My entire body goes cold, and I suddenly freeze, my body feeling like it's filled with cement.

Before I can do anything, he reaches out and grabs my wrist, yanking me inside with so much force, my bag flies off my arm, scattering the contents everywhere.

The sudden motion is a shock, but one my system needs to remind my brain to fight back. I try to pull my arm away, but he's too strong.

I scream, hoping someone will hear me.

"Ah. The sister," Mark says with a sneer, his eyes filled with so much hatred. "This was way easier than I ever could've imagined."

No. No. No. This can't be happening.

We were all so worried about Zoey's safety, I let my guard down about the possibility that I might be in danger too. I had been with Zoey when she'd confronted Mark, and I never thought he'd come after me because my mind doesn't think like a criminal or a madman.

I struggle against his grip as he talks. His strength is no match for my tiny arms, and my gun is lying ten feet away, along with the rest of my things from inside my bag.

Everything Oliver said is true. I am an easy mark on social media. Anyone can get to me and lure me to their house, and today, that someone is Mark. The gun gave me the illusion of safety, but it does me no good when I actually need it.

"Let me go," I beg, yanking my arm backward, but his grip is too tight on my wrist.

I took basic classes in self-defense, but in this moment, when fear grips my insides, I can't remember a damn lesson.

"Please."

Mark laughs like it's a game. "Not on your life, baby," he says, and the last word makes my skin crawl.

I'm not only worried for my life, but what he'll do to me before he steals my last breath. I should've known better when Sarah, the person he was supposed to be, wanted a booking as early as possible.

Her social media presence wasn't big, but a quick glance over her posts and everything appeared to be okay. I searched the property online, and it was owned by a Sarah Newel, who obviously isn't Mark, but here he is.

"We're going to have some fun first."

My stomach twists, and every part of my body comes alive, screaming for me to get away from him.

He pulls me forward as I plant my shoes into the tile, trying to get the rubber soles to work in my favor. But even the rubber is no match for Mark's strength against the shiny floor.

I use my nails, digging them into the skin of his arm as he drags me deeper into the house. I pull them toward me, ripping open his skin enough to make him bleed.

"Fuck," he growls and stops moving.

For a moment, I think I have a small victory until he rears back, his fist clenched, and unleashes a blow against the side of my face.

Pain explodes behind my cheek, and everything goes gray, the colors of the foyer fading. Never in my life have I been hit that hard, and never in my face. I would've fallen backward, but his grip on my arm is too tight. As I lift my head and my vision returns, he hits me again before I have a chance to brace myself.

But this time, nothing is gray, and everything goes dark.

My face throbs as I come to. Panic grips my insides as I realize where I am and who's with me. I don't dare open my eyes. Not yet. I do a quick check, listening for the sound of Mark near me, but I hear nothing. My clothes are still on, which is a relief, but everything else about my current situation has my heart beating double time.

How long have I been out?

Is anyone coming to get me?

I know Oliver will, but it could be hours, and I don't know how many minutes I have left.

Mark isn't sane. That much, I knew. No man does what he did to my sister and then goes through all the trouble to lure me here if they're of sound mind.

Never in my wildest dreams did I think he could be a murderer when we were standing in his place as Zoey told him to drop the charges. But the fact that he could punch me in the face twice without a second thought has me thinking I was wrong about him. He's way more dangerous than I ever could've imagined.

"You're awake," he says, his voice way too close to me. "You snore."

I'm horrified to hear I snore. No one has ever told me that, but I push it out of my mind right now because it's not important. I thought by staying still, he wouldn't know whether I was still knocked out. I was wrong.

"I texted your bitch sister," he says, "but she has my number blocked."

I will my eyes to open, but the right side is too swollen to be any good. "Don't hurt her."

He laughs, and the sound sends goose bumps

skittering across my skin. "The bitch deserves whatever she's going to get."

Man, this guy hates women. There's no one sweeter than Zoey, and although she told him to drop the charges, he is the one who violated her. She's the victim, not him.

"What did she ever do to you?" I ask, figuring if I can keep him talking, he'll have less time to hurt me.

"She's a whore."

I do another body inventory, realizing my hands are bound and I'm lying on a couch as he sits on a coffee table next to me.

The look on his face is nothing short of terrifying. He has a wicked gleam in his eyes, one I didn't see the last time I saw him. Mark is good-looking and has probably lured in way too many women with that face, making them all live a nightmare by making the wrong decision to sleep with him.

"Zoey's not a whore," I argue. I know I should keep my mouth shut for my own safety, but I can't let him talk about my sister that way without speaking up to defend her. "She's a good girl."

His laugh is deep and sinister, making my goose bumps grow larger. "That bitch wouldn't know good if it hit her in the face." He reaches out, running the pad of his index finger along the top of my hand. "But I bet you do. I have a feeling you're a very good girl, Lulu."

My stomach threatens to spill its contents, but somehow, I keep everything down.

Do not freak out.

Do not freak out.

Do not freak out.

I keep repeating the statement inside my head, but it doesn't help an ounce to tamp down the fear that's taken root deep in the pit of my stomach.

"Don't touch me," I tell him, pulling my hands away from his.

"Or what?" he says, scooting to the edge of the coffee table, closing the space between us.

"Or today's the last day you'll taste freedom," I promise him, hoping Oliver will be here soon.

"I'd rather taste you first," he says.

And with that, I freak the fuck out.

CHAPTER 18
OLIVER

THE BUILDINGS PASS by in a blur as I race toward the location of Lulu's cell phone. I've had to break fifty traffic laws on the drive, but nothing can stop me from getting to her as quickly as possible, especially a speeding ticket.

My phone rings, and Zoey's name flashes on my dash. I answer the call, keeping my eyes trained on the road. "Hey."

"Where are you?"

"Heading toward her."

"How far out?"

"Five miles."

"My dad and uncles are on the way too. I gave them the address. Do you think she's okay?"

"I don't know, sweetheart," I tell her, and the truth of those words guts me.

"Maybe she's just too busy with the client to check her phone."

"Yeah, maybe." But I know that's not the case. She would never go hours and hours without checking her phone. She uses it for everything. She told me the calculator is one of her most-used apps.

"I hate her job," Zoey says, surprising me.

"Me too, Zoey. When I get her back safe and sound, we're going to have a real conversation about it."

"That'll go over big," she says. "Oliver?"

"Yeah?"

"I'm really scared," she whispers.

"Me too, Zoey. Me too," I tell her, squeezing the steering wheel tighter as the fear grips my insides.

I roll through a stop sign, the final turn before getting to my destination, and I see Lulu's car parked in a driveway. "I'm here. I'll be in touch soon."

"Go get our girl, Oliver."

"On it," I tell her as I throw the truck into park. "Got to go."

"Bye," she says with a voice so tight she squeaks out the word.

I haul ass, running faster than I ever did in basic training, and head toward the front door. I can't plow inside, although every fiber in my body wants me to use my shoulder to pop the door open.

I stare up, listening to every sound around me. No footfalls are audible from the other side. No voices coming from within. If everything were on the up-and-up, someone would've at least shouted that they were coming to the door.

I knock again in case they didn't hear me the first time and press the button next to the door three times. There's no way anyone couldn't hear me unless they are purposely ignoring my presence. I count to ten, giving the person inside plenty of time to get to me.

One.

Two.

Three.

Four.

Five.

I take a deep breath, readying myself.

Six.

Seven.

Eight.

My body tightens, and I turn my shoulder toward the door.

Nine.

Ten.

I push forward with all my might, slamming my shoulder into the thick wood, and it pops open.

Flimsy construction is normally a bad thing, but today, I'm thankful their builder didn't use better materials.

"Lulu!" I shout as I stand in the foyer, my gaze moving around the expansive space.

I hear a scream in the distance, and my head

snaps in that direction. It's Lulu, and my heart sinks, making my heart pick up its pace.

My feet move on their own, my body propelled by the knowledge that she's alive and is, in fact, in danger.

I fucking knew it.

I take the steps two at a time, and as soon as my boots touch the top landing, a man steps out of one of the bedrooms. Not just any man either.

Mark.

My insides instantly turn to stone.

His face still hasn't completely healed and is a mess, but I am about to add to his pain.

The sunshine glints off something in his hand, and I realize he isn't going to fight with his fists. The man has a knife, but that doesn't scare me.

"You fucking piece of shit," I say as I barrel forward, ready to stop him from breathing.

He comes at me with the knife raised high above his head. Amateur. The man clearly doesn't know how to fight and has taken all his knowledge from movies.

I raise my arm, easily stopping his downward motion with the knife, and use my knee to pop him in the stomach. He lurches forward, sucking in air as my knee lodges in his insides.

I work quickly, slamming my fist down on his arm, causing his grip on the knife to loosen enough to send it sliding across the hardwood floor.

But the guy doesn't give up. He comes at me again, thinking he can inflict damage with his hands. We've done this dance before. He lost then, and he'll lose now.

I crouch down, popping up with all my might when he's close to me. My hands find his middle, and I thrust him into the air, tossing him to the side. Our location does the work for me, sending Mark over the railing of the top floor.

When he lands, the sound of bone cracking against the tile below makes me recoil. Not because I feel bad that his body is a mangled mess, but the crunch is something I've never heard before and I don't think I'll ever forget.

"Oliver!" Lulu screams from down the hall.

I stare at Mark for a moment, but he isn't moving. There's not a sound coming from him. He could be dead, but at this point, it doesn't matter to me. I hope he is. If I go to jail for saving Lulu's life, so be it. At least she'll be safe, and Mark will be out of their lives forever. I could sleep easy at night even if I were behind bars.

"Lulu!" I yell back as I hustle down the hallway.

"Oliver!" she yells again, but louder this time.

My hands shake as I turn the knob, not sure of how I'm going to find her inside. When the door opens, my boots stick to the floor as my mind comprehends what I see.

"Fuck," I groan, willing my body to move.

Tears stream down her swollen face as the rest of her body trembles.

I rush to her side, untying her hands before pulling her into my arms. "I've got you," I tell her, cradling her against my chest. "I've got you, sweetheart. You're safe now."

Lulu collapses against me, gripping my shirt in her small hands as her entire body shakes. "I thought he was going to kill me."

I squeeze my eyes shut, rocking back and forth with her in my arms. If he isn't already dead, he is going to be.

I want to check her out, make sure there aren't any wounds that I can't easily see. But she is too attached to me. It is too soon for me to pull away.

"You're safe," I reassure her as she cries in my arms. "He'll never hurt you again."

She tips her head back, and I peer down at her as her swollen red eyes meet mine. "He didn't…"

She doesn't need to finish the statement for me to know what she was going to say.

"He didn't rape me," she continues. "I fought him off the best I could."

By the looks of her face, I'd say she put up one hell of a fight and Mark wasn't gentle with her either. "You did good, baby. Real good."

"Lulu." Her father's voice fills the space.

She stiffens in my arms.

"It's okay, Lulu. Zoey called them."

"Fuck," she bites out. "He's going to lose his mind."

"He'll be in good company," I tell her, pressing my lips to her forehead.

A moment later, her father is in the doorway of the room we're sitting in.

"Jesus," he mutters as his eyes scan Lulu's face.

"It's not as bad as it looks, Dad," she tells him, somehow trying to console him at a time when we need to be comforting her.

He's on his knees in front of us a second later, reaching up to cup her face. "Lemme see, baby."

She pulls away from me only far enough for him to get a good look.

He winces as he sees both sides, a matching pair of swollen, discolored eyes, puffy cheeks, and a fat lip.

"I will kill him," Lucio seethes.

"I think I already did that," I tell him.

He peers up at me only for a moment before he looks back over his daughter's face. "He's still breathing, but not for long."

"No," Lulu snaps. "I want him to go to prison. Don't kill him."

Never in my life have I thought I'd be in this position. I never thought someone would be begging me to save another man's life, especially someone who deserved not to draw another breath.

"Lulu," her father whispers as he brushes the

underside of her cheek with his thumb. "Do you want to go through a trial?"

"Dad, are we really talking about him disappearing?"

"Your grandpa is here," her dad says.

"No. He needs to be alive," she replies. "Don't let them handle him. Please, Daddy."

"Fuck," her dad says, pushing himself up and hauling his ass back into the hallway. "Let him live."

"Why the fuck would we do that?" a man asks, and I'm not sure which one because I haven't spent enough time with them to know their voices.

"Lulu wants him to go to prison. Call the cops," Lucio tells them.

"Fucking bullshit," another man mutters.

"Just fucking do it," Lucio barks down at them.

"What a mess," she says as she curls her face back into my chest, and she tightens her fingers in the soft cotton material of my shirt. "I'm an idiot."

"No. You're not," I tell her, holding her as tightly as I can without hurting her. "You believe in the good in people, where I only see the bad."

"But you were right."

"I didn't want to be, sweetheart."

"I'm sorry."

I pull back, lifting her chin with my fingers. "Look at me, Lulu," I say when she doesn't open her eyes right away.

"What?" she says, her eyes barely visible through the swelling.

"This isn't your fault."

"It is."

"It's not. I love that you see good in everything and everyone. Not everyone is like Mark."

"I can never trust anyone again."

"Do you trust me?"

"Yes," she breathes as tears start streaming down her cheeks again.

"I love you, Lulu." It's the first time I've said those words to her. And I mean every single one too.

I'd never been so panicked in my entire life as I was today when I knew something had happened to her.

"I love you too, Oliver."

I lean forward, pressing my lips as gently as possible to her mouth.

This isn't how I wanted to say that to her.

I wanted it to be some grand romantic gesture by candlelight or some other fairy-tale bullshit. But this moment is too important not to tell her how I feel.

"I will always protect you," I promise her as soon as the kiss ends. "Always."

She curls back into me, melting against my chest. I know her wounds will heal, but the memories of this day will never fade. All I can do is help her move beyond the fear that piece of shit has now instilled in her and hope that I haven't lost the funny, carefree woman I fell for the moment I laid eyes on her.

CHAPTER 19
LULU

"MA'AM, THE PARAMEDICS ARE HERE," a female officer says as I'm curled in Oliver's arms.

"Come on, sweetheart." Oliver's deep voice makes my eyes close, but the moment of serenity is short-lived as he moves. "You need to be looked at by someone."

"Do I really?" I groan as he slides his arms under my legs and behind my back before he lifts me.

"Yes." He cradles me as he makes his way out of the room where I thought I'd take my last breath.

"I'm fine. Can't we just go home?"

"Don't argue," my dad says somewhere behind us, and I feel like a little kid, pleading for something I know I'll never get, but that doesn't stop me from trying.

"I just need some sleep," I whisper as the

exhaustion from today and the comfort of Oliver's arms threatens to pull me under.

A moment later, I'm set down in a chair in the living room. I can barely focus through the tiny slits of my eyes. They're so swollen, I'm surprised I can even see at all. I haven't looked in a mirror yet, but by the looks everyone has given me, I can tell it's bad.

The medic shines a light in my eyes, asking me a million questions. I answer the best I can, but my nerves are so frazzled, thinking is challenging.

"We need to take her in for some tests," the man says, but he isn't talking to me.

"Do whatever you need," Dad answers. "If something happens to her…"

"I'm fine, Daddy," I tell him.

"I'll go with her," Oliver says to him. "I'll keep her safe."

I never felt like those words were true coming from anyone's mouth besides my father's. But when it comes to Oliver, I can feel them deep in my bones.

"We'd like to get a statement," someone says, and I turn my head in their direction.

A cop.

"You can do it at the hospital," the medic tells him. "She needs to be tested for a concussion or any other issues before she can give you information."

"That's fine," the officer says. "We'll send a detective there to talk to her after the testing is done."

I slump over, wanting nothing more than to run away and slip under the comfy covers of my bed.

"We're going to need to talk to you too," the officer says, but he isn't staring at me now.

I peer up, finding Oliver standing at my side, the person the cop is talking to now.

"Not a problem. Is he alive?" Oliver asks the officer, squeezing my shoulder without looking at me.

"He is, he's in bad shape."

I'm so torn. Part of me wants the man to die. That's the sinister part. I've never been that girl, but being targeted and attacked changed that in me. But there's another part of me that wants to see Mark rot in prison for the rest of his miserable life. It's more satisfying and lengthier.

"He's already loaded and ready to roll," the medic tells the cop. "For right now, he's stable."

"Good," the officer replies. "Homicides are more paperwork."

I'm taken aback by the callousness for a moment, but it shouldn't be surprising.

"Ready?" another man asks, rolling in a gurney.

"I can walk," I tell them, not wanting to be treated like I'm helpless. I spent hours fighting off a man who wanted nothing more than to end my life and torture me.

"No can do, little lady. You're getting the special ride all our customers get," he says with a sweet smile.

I grumble under my breath, and I hate that I don't have a choice. "Can we at least skip the needles?"

The man's smile widens. "I'll see if I can pull a few strings."

I push myself up and try to stand, but everything starts to spin. Oliver grips my arm, holding me steady before my knees have a chance to crumple underneath me. "I've got you," he says as I give him my weight and lean on him for support.

Oliver doesn't let go of me until I'm on the gurney, ready for a ride I never wanted to take.

"Thank you," I tell him, smiling up at him—or at least I think I am, but with my lips as swollen as they are, who knows what expression I'm really giving him.

"I'm not leaving your side, sweetheart."

"Vinnie will drive your truck to the hospital," Dad tells Oliver. "We'll meet you two there."

Great. The entire gang is coming. I'm sure by the time we pull out of the driveway, the entire family will know what happened and will show up at the hospital.

Oliver fishes his keys out of his pocket, handing them off to my uncle. "Thank you."

"Take care of our girl," my uncle says to him.

"Been trying to, but she doesn't make it easy," Oliver replies.

"She's been like that since she was a little girl," Dad says before bending over and placing a soft kiss on my cheek. "We'll be right behind you, kiddo."

"Okay, Daddy," I whisper, feeling like a little kid again.

"And we're on the move," the medic says as someone starts to strap me down.

"Why?" I ask.

"So you don't fly around the back. It's a seat belt," he tells me, like it's the most logical thing in the world.

Everything passes by in a blur as they rush me out the front door with Oliver somewhere behind us. It's not the smoothest ride ever. The gurney needs a pair of shocks because every bump in the cement walkway is more jarring than some of Chicago's biggest potholes.

I'm placed in the back of the ambulance, followed by one of the paramedics and Oliver.

"How far?" Oliver asks the guy as he reaches for my hand, which, thankfully, isn't strapped down like the rest of me.

"Four minutes. And with Jessie driving, possibly three," he says, moving around the bay in the back to grab at some cords. "Just hooking you up. No needles."

"Thank you," I tell the man. I'm not an easy stick, and there's nothing I hate in this world more than being poked repeatedly.

The guy isn't lying about Jessie. It feels like he's driving a race car track rather than the sleepy roads of the northern suburb.

Oliver's hand tightens in mine as we take a corner so fast, my entire body stiffens.

"He's trying to make it in two point five," the man reading the machines on the opposite side of Oliver says.

"I think he's going to make it," Oliver replies, giving me a smile. "You okay?"

"Yeah," I say, but I'm lying.

Now that I've had a little bit of time, everything is starting to hurt. The rush and fear of earlier has dissipated, and I'm feeling more than I want to.

Once we arrive, the doctors and nurses are quick to assess me and get me into testing. Other than what's visible on the outside, there's no internal damage.

Oliver's with me when a new police officer arrives. "Good evening," he says, and it suddenly dawns on me that the entire day has passed between the attack by Mark and my time here at the hospital. "I'm Detective Larson. I need to ask you a few questions about what happened today."

"Sure," I tell him, wincing as I push myself up straighter, and every muscle and joint in my body protest.

"Can this wait?" Oliver asks the detective.

"We need to get everything while it's fresh in her mind and yours too."

"I'm good," I tell Oliver, squeezing his hand. "I need to tell someone what happened. I need to make sure he doesn't do this to anyone else. But—" I turn my gaze toward the detective "—the story is long."

"Take all the time you need."

I spend a ridiculous amount of time going into detail about what happened to Zoey and how Mark lured me to the house with a fake social media account. I tell the officer everything as best as I can remember under the circumstances.

"Is he okay? Mark," I ask.

"He's still in stable condition. His legs are broken, along with one arm. He has a concussion too, but it looks like he'll survive. We'll be placing him under arrest before he leaves the hospital."

"Thank God," I say and finally release a long, deep breath for the first time in hours.

"And me?" Oliver asks.

"And you what?" the detective asks.

"You know…" Oliver glances down at me as I meet his eyes, pleading with him to shut up.

"No charges are going to be filed against you for rescuing her. You're a hero in my book."

He's my hero too.

"Really?" Oliver's voice is as surprised as I feel at that revelation.

"I'm not even going to be taken down to the precinct?"

"Do you want to be?" Detective Larson asks.

"He's good," Grandpa says, walking into the room, looking every bit as calm and collected as he always does. "Thanks for your quick and hard work on this case, Detective."

If I didn't know better, I'd think my grandfather already made calls to everyone he knows in the area to make sure there'll be no blowback on Oliver.

"Here's my card," the detective says as he fishes one out of his jacket pocket and holds it out to me. "If you think of anything else, please don't hesitate to contact me. I'll be in touch soon to gather the evidence from your phone about the perpetrator."

"Thank you," I tell him as I hand the card to Oliver, having nowhere to store it since they made me wear this ridiculously flimsy hospital gown.

"Mr. Gallo," the detective says, giving my grandfather a chin dip before he strides out.

I knew it. He made calls. I'm not surprised, though. Sometimes it feels like my grandfather knows everyone in the city and all the surrounding suburbs. His earlier years, although tumultuous, are more than paying dividends now.

A second later, my dad is in the room with my mom on his arm. Her eyes widen the moment they land on my face.

"That bad, huh?" I ask her, trying to make light of the situation.

My mom isn't known for keeping her shit together when it comes to Zoey and me, and I have a feeling no matter what I do, she is going to lose it.

"Baby," she says, unlatching her arm from my dad and rushing to the side of my makeshift bed. "Jesus."

"He wasn't there," I tell her, making a funny.

She doesn't crack a smile as her gaze moves around my face, soaking it all in. "You look…" She winces as the words die in her throat.

"I know I look like shit, Ma."

"It'll heal," she says to me.

"You have to be in pain," she says, brushing a few strands of hair away from my forehead with a featherlight touch.

"They gave me the good stuff." I give her a lopsided smile. "I'm feeling nothing right now."

Her lips flatten. "How can you be cracking jokes at a time like this?"

"Ma."

"Lulu."

"Ma, come on. I'm okay. A few weeks of healing and I'll look like me again."

Her eyes shimmer with unshed tears. "I don't know what I would've done if something…"

"I'm okay," I tell her to stop those tears from making their way down her face. "If you cry, I'll cry."

She brushes the backs of her knuckles across the corner of her eye. "It's okay to cry, tough girl."

"I know, but it'll hurt like a bitch."

She groans, still not liking my attitude. But what else is new. I've tested my mother my entire life, and so has my sister, for that matter. "Always difficult."

"I'm your baby. Of course I am."

"Can she go home?" Ma asks Oliver.

"Yeah."

"I'm going to *my* home," I tell her, already knowing where she's going to lead the conversation before she has a chance to say it.

"I can take care of you," she says as my father slides his hand onto her shoulder, and she lifts her hand and places it on top of his.

"I'm going to go to my place. Zoey can take care of me."

"No," Oliver says, making my head turn up to meet his gaze. "I'll take care of you at your place, sweetheart. You're doing nothing until you're well again."

"Well, I…" I'm not about to argue with that. I like the sound of it, honestly, but I'm not sure how long I'll let them treat me like I'm an invalid before I lose my mind.

"Is that what you want?" Mom asks me.

"I want Oliver to stay with me," I tell her, but I keep my eyes on him. "He'll make sure I'm okay."

"Baby, let him take care of our girl."

"My girl," Oliver corrects them, and Dad doesn't even flinch, which is shocking as hell.

Ma rises to her feet and moves around the bed until she's in front of Oliver. "Thank you," she says to him, placing her hand on the middle of his chest.

"You saved her, and for that, I'll forever be in your debt."

"You owe me nothing, Mrs. Gallo," Oliver says so sweetly that tears start to form in my eyes.

Damn it.

"Where is she?" my grandma says, rushing into the room with Zoey next to her. "Oh my God. My baby." Grandma pushes my dad aside like he weighs nothing and gapes at me. "Dear Lord."

"I'm okay," I say for what feels like the hundredth time today.

"Lulu," Zoey whispers, covering her mouth with her hand.

"It looks worse than it feels," I tell my sister, but again, I'm lying. I have no idea how bad it really looks because no one has given me a mirror to use.

"Have you seen it?" Zoey asks me.

"No mirror."

She shakes her head. "Your phone has a camera, Lulu."

Fuck. I forgot. I could've easily turned on the camera to check out what Mark did to me.

"But I'd wait a day because it's not pretty."

"It'll look worse tomorrow," Grandpa says, and all eyes in the room turn to him with a pointed glare. "What? It's true. It'll look worse as it heals."

"Shut up, Tino," Gram says to him with a backhanded swat to his chest. "You're not helping."

"This is all my fault," Zoey says as she comes to

the side of the bed and lifts herself up, planting one ass cheek next to my legs.

I scoop her hand in mine. "It's not your fault. Stop that, sissy."

She can't bring herself to look at me. "But it is."

"This is Mark's fault," I tell her. I'll never blame my sister for the choices a madman made.

"I brought him into our lives."

"Don't let the actions of one asshole ruin your life, Zo. Not everyone is like Mark. There are good ones out there. Look at Oliver," I tell her, thinking back over all the ways he's saved me since the day I met him on the side of the highway.

"Olivers are rare," she whispers.

I worry my sister's broken and will never easily trust another man again. Mark stole that from her, but I will do everything in my power to keep him from stealing her entire future. Zoey deserves happiness. She deserves love. She deserves a man who will treat her like a queen and protect her from everyone, even if it's from her own decisions sometimes.

"There are more Olivers than Marks," Dad says to Zoey. "But maybe dating apps aren't the best way to find them."

"No one thinks they're actually going to *date* someone off those apps," I say before I think through the statement.

Zoey's eyes widen, and I realize my mistake immediately.

"Fuck," Dad mutters, swiping a hand down his face as he spews out a string of curse words behind his palm.

"Anyway, can I bust out of this place yet?"

"I'll go find the doctor," Gram says, rushing from the room faster than she entered.

"She's okay," Gram says to whoever else is in the hallway. "She's ready to go. Can someone make that happen?"

"On it," Uncle Vinnie tells her.

"I'm ready to go home and sleep." I peer up at Oliver again. Why does the man have to be so damn tall? If my neck didn't hurt before, it sure as hell does now. "I could use a shower too."

"A bath," he says to me. "You need to relax those muscles in some warm water for a while."

"I'll make us dinner too," Zoey adds. "If I can stay the night."

"Stay as long as you want," I say to her.

"Maybe tomorrow, we can do a movie night." She smiles and turns her eyes toward Oliver.

"What movie?" he asks in that grumbly voice.

"*Steel Magnolias*."

"Action movie?" he asks her.

"Nope."

"Damn it," he snaps.

Zoey breaks out into a fit of giggles, and I know everything's going to be okay.

CHAPTER 20
OLIVER

I WALK into the bathroom and find Lulu in front of the mirror.

"It's worse than I thought," she says, staring at me in the reflection.

I come up behind her and wrap my arms around her shoulders, meeting her gaze. I wish I could erase the day and everything that happened to her. "You always look beautiful."

She steps backward and leans against me, resting her head on my shoulder. "You clearly need glasses, Oli."

"Eyesight's perfect, sweetheart."

"I do look kind of badass, don't I?"

"Toughest woman I've ever seen."

"I've had a black eye before," she admits, peering up at me. "Only once and only one eye. First time having a matching set."

"What happened?" I ask, wanting to keep her mind off what happened today. She'll have time to process it all later, and I'll be there to pick up the pieces when she does.

"There was this mean girl at school who kept picking on Zoey. She would shit-talk her every day. Zoey would always walk home at the end of the day in tears. I could only take it for so long before I decided I would have a little talk with Marly. That's her name, Marly Milano."

"I'm guessing the talk didn't go well."

"Wrong."

"Then how did you end up with a black eye?" I ask, turning her around so I can undress her.

"What are you doing?" she asks as my fingers touch the bottom of her shirt.

"Taking care of you, and that starts with a bath."

"I can get undressed."

"You talk, I'll do the rest."

She stares at me for a second and I think she's about to argue, but she doesn't. "Marly was a talker, and I mean, the girl wouldn't shut up. She thought she could talk to me like she did to Zoey. I had none of it." She pauses for a moment as I lift her shirt over her head.

"Who made the first strike?"

"Marly attacked me with her mouth, so I introduced her to my fist."

I crouch down and work the button of her jeans. "Did she win?"

"Bite your tongue," she says, placing her hands on my shoulders to step out of her pants. "She got the first blow, but I got the last."

"Who looked worse?" I ask, keeping her talking as I toss her jeans to the floor where her shirt landed.

"Marly, of course."

"Did you get in trouble?"

"I got suspended from school because it was on their property."

"And your parents?"

"I was grounded for about two hours until they found out what Marly was doing to Zoey."

"Did the bullying stop after that?"

"Marly never spoke to Zoey again."

"What grade were they in?"

"Zoey was in sixth grade."

"Did Marly switch schools?"

"No."

"She didn't talk to her for eight years?" I ask as I take her hand, helping her toward the waiting tub.

"Nope. Marly was too scared of me to even risk upsetting Zoey again."

"I definitely got myself a tough girl."

"Not anymore, though," she says as she lifts a foot and holds on to my hand as she climbs into the tub. She hisses as she dunks her foot into the hot water. "It's no fun at my age to be this busted up."

"It doesn't get easier as you get older. At my age, I'm wrecked for days."

"When was the last time you were hit?"

I hold on to her until she's settled into the water. "It's been a long time. I think I'd just gotten out of the service and had a huge attitude problem."

"Shocker," she says as she pulls her knees toward her chest and rests her chin on top. "This feels good."

"You have blood in your hair." I rub the stiff ends between my fingers. "It needs to be washed."

"I'm too tired."

"I'll do it," I tell her. "Be right back."

She reaches out and grabs my hand. "Where are you going?"

"To grab a cup."

"Oh," she says, letting her hand slip away from mine.

I rush out of the bathroom and head to the kitchen, not wanting to leave her alone for long.

Zoey looks up from the pot of soup she's already started. "What's wrong?"

"I need a cup to wash her hair."

Zoey's eyebrows rise. "Want me to do it?"

I shake my head and grab a clean cup from the counter near the sink. "No. I got it. She was telling me about Marly."

Somehow, Zoey's eyebrows move higher. "She told you about Marly Milano?"

I nod. "Yeah."

"Lulu's had my back my entire life," she says, "I owe her more than a pot of soup."

"That's what family does, Zoey. I've got to go."

"I'll be here," she says and chews on her bottom lip as she goes back to working on the soup.

Lulu's eyes are closed when I walk back into the bathroom. She's sitting up, knees to her chin, looking bruised and battered, but not mentally beaten. "Zoey okay?" she asks, always worried more about her sister than herself, which seems to have been a theme for their entire lives.

"She's good. Cooking."

"Don't get your hopes up," she says, opening her eyes as I pull over a chair she has in the bathroom for some reason. "She's an awful cook."

"Great," I whisper, setting the cup on the edge of the tub. I grab a towel and the shampoo before I settle into the chair as close to her head as I can get without climbing into the tub with her. It's too small for two people, and with the shape she's in, I wouldn't dare try to sandwich myself in there with her. "I'm starving."

"Maybe we should call in a pizza. The bar will deliver it here."

"They will?" I ask as I dip the cup in the water.

"They will for me. It's one of the perks of being related to the owners."

"If the soup is bad, we'll order pizza."

"It'll taste like dirty dishwater."

"Ready?" I ask, ignoring the comment about the soup because I'm too hungry to think it'll be anything except delicious. I've had bad food. The meals served in the military are barely edible, but you either choke them down or starve.

"Yes," she says as she tips her head back and closes her eyes.

"I've never done this before, so I'm sorry in advance."

She reaches up, touching my arm as I hold the cup above her head. "Just go slow."

I do as she says, slowly pouring the water down the back of her head, using one hand to shield her eyes from any splash-over. When her hair is wet enough, I grab the shampoo, pouring a small amount into my hands.

"More," she says.

"You can't even see my hand."

"The squirt wasn't long enough."

Again, I don't argue with her. I could wash my hair with a bar of soap, and it would come out looking the same as it would with the most expensive shampoo.

Lulu moans as I work the shampoo into her hair, spending extra time on the ends where blood and whatever else has dried. "That feels so good," she says, her voice soft and sleepy.

I let the silence fill the room as I make more bubbles in her hair, far more than I ever do in my own. I can't imagine doing this every day. It must be exhausting. I could never handle being a woman.

"You're good at this."

"I'll wash your hair whenever you want," I tell her as I keep my gaze trained on her hair, trying my best to keep the suds from slipping down her forehead.

"I needed this," she says, letting go of a long exhale. "But I can't wait to go to sleep."

"Soon," I reply, grabbing the cup again. "Have to eat something."

"I don't need to add hangry to the list of things wrong with me tonight," she grumbles. "If the soup's shit, I'm going to have toast and crawl into bed."

"Whatever you want, sweetheart."

"Will you come with me?"

"To bed?"

"Yes," she says, tipping her hair back farther as I pour a cup full of water down the back of her head.

"There's nowhere else I'd rather be."

She reaches into the tub, fishing out a shower puff. "Can you hand me the shower gel?"

I grab a small bottle of pink liquid, hoping it is what she wants. "This?"

She turns her head toward my hand. "Yes," she says as she takes the bottle from my hand and pours a small amount into the ball. "I'm almost ready to get out. I'm getting hot in here."

I pour a few more cupfuls of water down her hair

until there are no more bubbles. "I'll grab some towels."

"In the cabinet near the sink," she says as she rubs the soap into her skin.

Her bathroom is extremely organized. It's not surprising that she chose it as a career. I'm lucky if I can find something after opening only two drawers in my bathroom.

"Grab two. I need one for my hair."

"Got it," I tell her as I grab two large towels from the cabinet exactly where she said they'd be. They were all perfectly folded into the same size, facing the same direction.

Lulu rinses the soap from her body as I take the seat behind her again with the towels in my lap. "Take your time."

"If I stay in here any longer, I'm going to pass out from the heat."

"Sorry," I tell her because I filled the tub.

"Don't be. I like it hot."

I figured as much. I didn't know a single woman who likes a lukewarm bath—or shower, for that matter. If the temperature doesn't match that of the surface of the sun, it isn't hot enough. I don't know if it's a hormonal issue, but there is a disconnect between males and females when it comes to temperatures of just about everything.

When she's finished, I help her stand and give her the towel to dry herself off.

"Do you want me to dry your hair?" I ask even if I don't have any idea how she does it.

"No. I'll let it air-dry."

"You're going to go to bed with wet hair?"

She lifts a shoulder. "I'm too tired to bother drying it."

"Again, I'll do it."

"No. It takes forever. I'll deal with the mess tomorrow."

"Okay," I say, unwilling to argue with her when we are so close to getting out of this virtual sauna.

When we finally make it out of the bathroom, Zoey has the table set and the pot of soup waiting in the middle. "I kept the pieces small."

"What is it?" Lulu asks as I pull out a chair for her.

"Your favorite."

"Ramen?" Lulu asks, peering into the pot.

Zoey nods. "But I put fresh veggies in it, so it's slightly healthy."

Lulu smiles at her sister. "It's perfect, Zo. This is a good way to end a shit day."

"So, it's edible, then?" I ask, earning looks from both of them.

"I know my limits, and it doesn't involve homemade soup," Zoey says, grabbing Lulu's bowl. "I'm great at ramen, though. It's one of the only things I can't screw up."

"Miracles do happen," Lulu says, touching her sister's arm as Zoey scoops out the long, curly noodles.

"I've had a lot of practice, and it's hard to mess up water, noodles, and their little magical packet of flavor."

I don't care what she made. I am going to eat enough to fill my stomach and then take Lulu to bed and put the entire day behind us. We'd deal with the fallout tomorrow or whenever Lulu is ready to talk about it in more detail.

Lulu and Zoey have a great relationship. They genuinely like each other. Liam and I have never had that. Sure, we love each other, but that's because we grew up together. However, Liam and I have never had the same closeness as the girls.

Would I go to battle for my brother? Hell yeah, but that doesn't mean I want to spend more time with him than I have to.

With every passing year, Liam has become a bigger shithead. My time in the military created the biggest wedge between us. I think Liam felt abandoned, and he's never been able to get over the years I was gone.

"How many times have Mom and Dad called?" Lulu asks, moving the vegetables around in her bowl.

I grab the ladle, filling my bowl halfway, not wanting to take any food away from the girls. My time will be spent staying quiet, letting them talk about whatever they want.

"More than you want to know," Zoey tells her. "They're worried, but I told them you were in good hands."

"Literally," Lulu says, giving me a sheepish smile as she lifts the spoonful of carefully rolled noodles to her mouth.

"Mom's beside herself that you didn't stay with them."

"I know," Lulu breathes, "but they'd hover. And right now, I need space."

"Do you want me to go?" Zoey asks, setting her spoon down in the bowl.

"No. No. I want you here. I need you here." Lulu glances at me. "You too."

"I'm wherever you need me," I promise her. "For as long as you do."

"I like this," Zoey says. "It's like having a brother."

"This is nice," Lulu says. "Not the other stuff, but this part."

"Yeah," Zoey says. "Do you ever wish we had a brother?"

"God no." Lulu's quick to answer. "It would've been awful. Boys are so smelly and annoying." She looks at me again. "Not you, of course, but the others."

"I have my moments," I tell her, trying to keep the conversation light.

"I think after me and you, they'd had enough.

The thought of another kid, especially a boy, would've sent them right over the edge," Zoey adds.

"We were a handful," Lulu says.

"Still are." Zoey snorts. "The last few days are a testament to that."

"Amen," Lulu says, laughing with her sister.

"Were you an easy child?" Zoey asks me.

"What do you think?" I reply.

Zoey shakes her head. "Not a chance."

"Liam was worse, but I was a handful too."

"Liam sounds like quite the character," Zoey says.

"He's not as bad as Oliver makes him out to be," Lulu tells Zoey.

"Yes, he is. You just haven't spent enough time with him," I reply.

"You haven't spent enough time with our cousins. We have some doozies," Zoey tells me.

"Everyone's been so nice," I say.

"They're on their best behavior around you. You'll see. They'll show their true colors soon enough."

"I look forward to it," I say to them, hoping to stick around long enough to know them as well as I know my own family.

CHAPTER 21
LULU

SIX MONTHS *Later*

The waves lap against the sand as the sun moves lower in the sky, hovering above the horizon. "This is paradise," I say, closing my eyes to feel the warmth of the last rays of the day.

"I can't imagine every day being like this," Oliver says on the blanket next to me.

"We can come down here whenever we want. It's one of the perks of having family here."

"Maybe we should become snowbirds."

I turn my head, letting my gaze linger on his tanned skin for far too long. "You want to get a place here?"

He pushes his sunglasses onto his head as he sits up, resting his weight on his elbows. "Something small, maybe."

"I like that idea, but are you sure? Winter is big business for you in Chicago."

"Liam's there, and we can hire someone to take my place when I'm out of town."

My smile widens because maybe we can pull this off. I've changed how I run my business since the incident with Mark.

I hired two employees and always have one of them with me when I'm working. No one is ever alone, so there's no chance of something like that happening again. Well, not no chance, but it wouldn't be as easy with another person in tow.

"The girls can handle the work while I'm gone too. Maybe we don't stay all winter, but we can pop down here for a few weeks at a time to warm our bones."

"I'm getting too old for the cold," Oliver says.

I roll onto my side and push myself up to straddle him. His hands find my thighs as I settle on top of him, pressing my middle to his. "You're not old, baby. You're well seasoned."

He chuckles, the vibration sending a spark through my body. "You like the splashes of gray, don't you?"

My fingers find the white hairs in his beard, toying with the strands. "It's distinguished."

"My girl," he whispers, his rough fingertips skating over my skin, sending goose bumps across my skin, which should be impossible in the oppressive Florida heat.

"I'm her."

"Mine. Only mine," he says as he pushes himself up to sitting, taking me with him.

I wrap my arms around his shoulders, hanging on as he shifts us to find a comfortable position. "I don't know what I did to get so lucky," I whisper against his lips as my gaze searches his.

"Lucky? You have a lack of self-preservation I had to keep saving you from."

"You are my hero. You know that."

"I know, and there's nothing else I'd want to be," he whispers back.

I press my mouth to his as the sun warms my skin. The only thing hotter is his palm against my back, holding me to him like a tether.

He pulls away, breaking the most perfect kiss. "Lulu."

"Yeah?" I ask as my eyes flutter open.

"I want to ask you something."

"Okay."

"Do you want this forever? Want me?"

My fingers graze the back of his neck, near the ends of his hair. "Of course."

"I want forever with you, sweetheart."

"Me too."

"I've never loved anyone the way I love you, and I

know you're it for me. I knew from the moment we met that my life would never be the same."

Oh my God. Oh my God.

My eyes widen as he holds a box between us. Not just any box, but a ring box covered in green velvet.

"I don't want to date anymore. I don't want you to be only my girlfriend. I want you to be my wife. I want forever with you. I want babies, lots of babies, and a family. I want to spend eternity here with you and beyond, if there's something else after this. Lulu Gallo, will you do me the honor of becoming my wife?"

"Oliver," I whisper as my vision blurs and my eyes fill with water.

I'd hoped this day would come. We haven't really talked much about the future, deciding to take things day by day. The last six months has been a roller coaster with the trial for Mark and waiting for there to be blowback against Oliver because sometimes the justice system is ass-backward.

"Yes," I say as I start to hyperventilate when the reality that Oliver's proposing washes over me. "I want that. I want all of that with you."

"I love you," he says, still holding the box and not opening it.

It doesn't matter if there is a bubble gum wrapper in the shape of a ring inside the box. None of that matters as long as he's my forever. The ring is decoration. A declaration to others that we're dedicated to each other. He's my everything.

"I love you too," I say and lunge forward, smashing my lips against his in the most ungentle way.

Oliver laughs before he kisses me back, but he takes it deeper, demanding more, and I give it to him. This is my man, my forever.

If you had asked me a year ago if I'd fall in love, I would've said no. I wasn't in the headspace, and every guy I'd met to that point had been a shithead who cared more about himself than anyone else, especially his girlfriend.

Oliver is the first man who isn't self-absorbed. He is the first one who wanted to make me happy, even if that meant putting himself second. I put him first, but he doesn't always do that for himself.

I've never felt safe with anyone else before. I don't think any of them would have jumped in front of a bullet for me. But Oliver would. He put himself in danger more than once to save my life, and I know he'd do it again without a second thought.

"The ring," he says against my lips.

"It doesn't matter," I tell him.

Oliver pulls his lips away, and his hand disappears from my back. "It does. I spent a small fortune on it." He pops the lid of the box open, revealing the ring.

My eyes grow wide as the diamond sparkles in the

setting sun. "It's beautiful," I whisper, getting choked up.

Oliver doesn't look like the type of man who could pick out something so pretty on his own. He looks like a solitaire guy. Something classic.

"Zoey helped me," he says, like he's reading my thoughts.

"She kept this a secret?" I ask, shocked because no one in my family can keep their mouth closed, and Zoey is sometimes the worst offender.

He pulls the ring from the box, holding it out for me. "She did. You like it?"

"Stunning." The diamond is a princess cut and has to be at least a carat. It's almost too big for my finger, but I'll wear the shit out of it. Not because it's obscenely big, but because it represents something I thought I'd never have...a forever.

"Someone looks happy," Aunt Izzy says as we walk into Inked, having booked a late-night tattoo session before we got to Florida.

"You're here late," I tell her, glancing around.

"I just stopped in to drop some things off to the kids."

I smile when she says kids. Her kids are grown and have their own, but I guess that's part of being a parent—your kids never really grow up to you.

I hold out my hand, showing off the flashy ring Oliver got me.

Izzy's eyes widen as soon as her gaze homes in on the bling. She reaches out, taking my hand to pull it closer to her face. "Oh my God, Lulu. Congrats, kid. And good job, Oliver."

"Thanks," Oliver says from behind me, standing so close I can feel his body heat that's only exacerbated from all the sunbathing today.

"I can't wait to come up to Chicago for the wedding."

"Oh God," I breathe, suddenly hit with the realization that we were going to have a big wedding. I like attention, but I'm not sure I can handle that many people at one time.

"Don't worry," Aunt Izzy says, giving my hand a squeeze. "Weddings are more fun than you think they'll be."

"Maybe we'll have it here on the beach," I tell her, turning to see Oliver's face to get his reaction.

"Whatever you want, sweetheart."

"Smart man," Aunt Izzy says, giving Oliver a smile. "You two tattooing your names on each other?"

"Oh, hell no," I tell her.

She laughs. "Good. Don't do that. Not ever. Got it?"

I nod. "Do people still do that?"

"Yep, but at least they're repeat customers when they come back for a cover-up."

"Hey. Hey. Sorry. I was cleaning up and prepping things for you two," Gigi, my cousin and another kickass chick, says as she walks out from the back area.

"I'm out," Aunt Izzy says. "James is waiting for me, and the man isn't patient anymore."

Gigi brushes her hair over her shoulder, always looking beautiful. I don't know how she does it. By this time of night, I resemble a train wreck, while she looks like she walked off the set of a photo shoot for a tattoo magazine. "Was he ever patient?"

"No," Aunt Izzy says as she grabs her purse and moves toward the door. "But his punishments have gotten more creative."

Gigi holds up a hand. "We don't want to know."

Izzy laughs as she pushes open the door and disappears into the darkness.

"Punishments?" I ask my cousin.

Gigi shakes her head. "You don't want to know about their creative sex life. I know way more than I ever wanted to. Trust me."

My eyebrows rise as I turn my gaze back toward the direction where Izzy just was. "Really?" I whisper.

"Wow," Oliver says, echoing my sentiment.

"They may be old, but they sure as hell don't act like it sometimes."

"Who's old?" Carmello, another cousin, asks as he walks out from where Gigi just was.

"Your parents," Gigi tells him.

"Yep."

"Your mom was just talking about your dad punishing her," I say to him, hoping to get more details because my aunt Izzy has always been a wild one and someone I looked up to when I was little.

Carmello's face turns pink. "They're too much sometimes. I wonder if they'll still be chasing each other around when they're eighty."

"I bet they will," Gigi says to him. "Especially if your dad has anything to say about it."

He holds up a hand and glances down at the floor. "I don't want to talk about their sex life anymore."

I don't blame him. The very thought of my parents doing it turns my stomach. But I know how Zoey got here and how babies are made. I had already been born when they met. It is a complicated story that my mom doesn't like to talk about much. The memories from her childhood are too painful for her because the man who's genetically my grandfather was a real piece of work.

I didn't even know Lucio wasn't my biological father until I was almost a teenager. He never treated me like I wasn't his. Zoey and I were equals in his eyes, and I never knew another father besides him. I am blessed to have him in my life and couldn't ask for a better dad.

"So, what are we doing?" Gigi asks, leaning against the counter. "You have a design?"

I reach into my pocket, grabbing my phone. "I have the artwork saved."

"Shoot it to me, and I can work it up real quick. And you?" she asks, looking over my shoulder at Oliver.

"She has it."

"Send them both to me. Pike is just finishing up, and he'll be ready by the time the final touches on the designs are finished. Are we doing black or color?"

"Color for me and black for him."

"Excellent," she says, clicking away at the computer screen as I send her the two designs via email.

"Got them," she says a second later. "Want some water or something while I work on these?"

I shake my head. "We're good."

"Have a seat and relax. We'll be ready soon."

I smile at my cousin and nod. "Got it."

Oliver takes my hand, pulling me toward the bank of chairs along the wall. I'm nervous. I don't know why. I have tattoos, but every time I get a new one, I feel an energy that buzzes through my system. Whether it's anticipation or fear, the feeling is one that puts me on edge.

"Relax," Oliver says, placing his hand on my knee that's bouncing up and down like it's connected to a motor somewhere.

I take a deep breath and close my eyes.

"You want to skip it?"

My eyes snap open. "No way. I want this."

"You don't look like it."

"This is how I always look before a tattoo."

"Man, I don't know if I'd get another one if I freaked out as much as you are right now."

"It's a good energy."

He laughs. "Sure, sweetheart. Whatever you say. You sure you want it on your hip?"

"Is it bad there?" I ask him because he has tattoos everywhere and knows which spots are more sensitive than others.

"Not any worse than anywhere else."

"Okay. Good." I take another deep breath, getting my heart rate to slow a bit.

"It's a good thing we leave tomorrow because sunshine and new tattoos don't mix," he says.

"Well then, it's a good thing we're about to roll into winter again."

"Fuck," he hisses. "I'm not ready."

"We'll come back after Christmas and maybe plan a destination wedding here."

"Perfect," he says, lifting my hand to his mouth and brushing his lips against the soft skin on top.

"It will be," I tell him, knowing the future we'll have together will be exactly that.

Absolute perfection.

CHAPTER 22
OLIVER

CHRISTMAS – *Clearwater, Florida*

"How can you look so calm?" Liam asks me, pacing around the room like a caged animal.

"Why wouldn't I be?"

He stops, spins on his heel, and pins me with his stare. "Because you're getting married."

"I asked her to marry me."

My brother drags a hand down his face as he shakes his head. "It's a big step. Nail in the coffin. End of it all."

"End of what?"

"Freedom," he says as he starts to pace again, wearing a path in the carpeting of the hotel room.

The door opens, and Vinnie pops his head in. "We're ready."

I give him a nod and turn toward the full-length mirror, making sure nothing is out of place as Vinnie disappears. "I'm ready." I move toward the door, but Liam stops me, grabbing my arm.

"Are you sure?"

"Brother, if I weren't sure, I wouldn't have asked her. What's your problem?"

He drops his hand and tucks it into the pocket of his pants. "I thought... I don't know. I thought you'd be single your entire life."

"I didn't have plans to get married anytime soon, but when you meet the right girl, you got to make sure the relationship sticks."

"I like Lulu," he says.

"Well, that's good. Didn't matter if you didn't."

"She's perfect for you."

"I know."

"But I'm sure someone thought Mom and Dad were perfect for each other before they were married, and look at how they turned out."

I place my hand on Liam's shoulder, trying to console my brother. "Not every relationship ends like theirs, Liam. I won't let their mistakes guide my future. I want to be married to Lulu. I want to make a family. I want however many years I have left on this planet with the woman I love."

"Will I still be your family?" he asks, his lips turned down as he can barely meet my gaze.

"You'll always be my family. You're not losing a brother. You're gaining a sister."

"Fuck. I never wanted one of those. They're so bossy."

"My sons," Mom says, stepping into the room before I have a chance to leave.

Everyone is waiting downstairs, and the wedding is set to start in fifteen minutes. The sunset won't wait for anyone, especially my family and their relationship issues.

"You both look so handsome," she says, touching Liam's cheek before kissing mine.

"Can we walk and talk?" I ask her, glancing down at my watch.

"Oh yes. We can't be late," she replies and walks back toward the door.

I take my mom's arm as soon as we're in the hallway, the door slamming behind us. I hate hotels. It's impossible to get any sleep because everything needs to seal shut like it's Fort Knox.

"Are you nervous?" Mom asks.

"Not a bit, but he is." I tick my chin in Liam's direction.

"He's always a bundle of energy. He has been since the day he was born. Sometimes good, but usually bad."

"I can hear you," Liam gripes, smashing his finger into the elevator button.

"Maybe he'll get married soon," Mom says.

Liam turns and shakes his head. "Not a chance. I'm too young for that."

"Too dumb too," I add, teasing my brother.

"Sharla doesn't want to get married either," he adds.

"Sharla isn't the type of woman you marry," Mom tells him, saying what we all think but don't say. "But you're not the type of man a woman wants to marry either."

"What's that mean?" Liam asks her as the elevator doors open.

We step inside and I hope the conversation is going to end, but of course it doesn't.

"You're too into a good time. You party too much, and you're more led around by the thing between your legs than what's in that head of yours."

"Oh, his head leads him, just not the right one," I say, thinking I'm being cute, but the look my mother gives me says otherwise.

"I'm too young," Liam says, jamming his finger against the lobby button harder than he did to get the elevator to our floor. "Give me ten years."

"You'll be in your forties then," Mom says, shaking her head.

"My life will be almost over at that age. Might as well settle down before everything stops working."

"Jesus," Mom mutters. "Nothing stops working then."

"Pretty much," Liam adds.

"You're going to look like a grandpa at your kid's high school graduation," Mom tells him.

Liam winces. "I'm never having children. A wife is bad enough, but babies? Hell no."

I roll my eyes. I don't know why he's so sour on everything. Sure, our parents weren't the epitome of romance and a long-term relationship. But our lives weren't that bad, and we were along for the ride with Randall and Mom, who have a good relationship.

As soon as the elevator doors open, the music from the beach and the string quartet Lulu booked hits me. My heart leaps in my chest as I step into the warmth and humidity, and everything crashes into me.

I'm getting married today.

I am lucky enough to have found an amazing woman, but the fact that she is willing to hitch her trailer to me forever is a freaking miracle.

She is all class, while I am covered in oil and smell like burned rubber.

I've never been the type to get nervous in front of a crowd, but when I walk down the aisle toward the officiant and everyone turns to look at me, my stomach dips.

Lulu's mom stops me before I can take my place. "You look so handsome, Oliver. You doing okay, baby?"

"I'm good, ma'am." I give her a smile, seeing Lulu's features in her face.

"I'm not a ma'am to you. I'm Delilah or Ma.

That's it," she says and lifts her hand to my tie, adjusting it. "Got it?"

"I do," I say as I lift my gaze toward the bank of elevators I just came from.

"Treat my baby good, and we won't have an issue."

"I plan to worship her."

She smiles up at me and pats my chest. "Welcome to the family, Oliver."

I realize then, I'm not only marrying Lulu—I am joining something bigger. I never had a large family, at least not one I was close to by distance or familiarity. They say when you marry someone, you marry their family, and there's no other group of people I'd rather join than the Gallos. They are solid people. Welcoming and kind. Gracious and giving. Nosy and sweet. They don't have a bad side that I've seen, and they are more than willing to have one another's backs for just about anything, even if it puts their lives in danger.

"Go," my soon-to-be mother-in-law says, pushing me toward my spot on the beach where I'll watch my future walk toward me.

I have barely a moment to catch my breath and ready myself when the elevator doors slide open, and the music the quartet is playing changes.

My breath lodges in my throat as Lulu steps out of the elevator and is bathed in sunshine like an angel coming down from the heavens.

"Damn," I whisper, knowing I'm the luckiest son of a bitch in the world. On paper, we don't work, but when we are together, nothing else matters.

She is the clean to my messy. She is the organized to my chaos.

"Stunning," I say, unable to take my eyes off her as she glides down the sand toward me on her father's arm.

The attendants stand, turning in her direction.

We lock eyes, and everything else fades away. My wife is walking toward me.

My wife.

My future.

Never in a million years did I think I'd meet my future that day I took the call about a busted tire. I almost passed the job to Liam. And if I had, I wouldn't be here, and Lulu may very well not be alive because there's no way he would've tackled her to save her life.

All the nervousness I've had about standing up in front of everyone vanishes as she stops before me, looking more beautiful than I've ever seen her look in my life.

"Hi," she says with a slight squeak to her voice.

"Hi," I whisper, trying not to have my voice crack since I'm getting all choked up.

I've never been an emotional guy, but there's something about this moment that makes it impossible for me to keep my shit even.

"You're beautiful," I mouth as the officiant starts to talk, and everyone behind us sits.

The ceremony passes in a blur. I can't stop staring at the woman of my dreams whom I somehow made my reality. I don't know what I did to deserve this kind of happiness, but I'm thankful for it every single day.

When the man says, "You may kiss the bride," I grab my wife and pull her flush against me.

I see a hunger burning in her eyes as I lean down and take her lips with mine. The kiss isn't sweet and gentle like they show in those shitty movies Lulu and Zoey force me to watch with them. No. This is a claiming. A marking. I kiss her long and deep, leaving my mark and sealing the union forever.

Lulu's breathless as I pull away from her, and our family and friends clap, along with a few hoots and hollers.

We did it.

We are officially husband and wife.

"I love you," I tell my wife.

"I love you too, husband," she says, sending a thrill of pleasure through me.

"Say it again," I tell her, holding her around the waist.

"Husband," she whispers, peering up at me with so much love, my heart threatens to burst.

"Let's get this party started," Zoey says, breaking the moment, which is probably for the best because I was about ready to throw Lulu over my shoulder and consummate the marriage immediately.

"I'm starving," Lulu says.

"Me too, but not for food."

Lulu smiles up at me, placing a hand on my chest. "Later, big guy. We have a party to attend, and we're the guests of honor."

"Can we leave early?"

"All good things come to those who wait."

I've waited my entire life for this moment. I can wait a little longer. Celebrating our big day is important to Lulu—and me too—but she planned every little detail, and I want everything to be perfect for her. She deserves as much.

I take my wife's hand, leading her back down the aisle as our guests move in front of us, heading toward the terrace overlooking the beach at sunset.

The only thing more beautiful than a sunset over the Gulf is my wife, and I do my best to memorize every moment of today to look back on someday when I am old and my body is wrinkled.

"Huh," Zoey says, glancing over at my brother as they walk a few feet in front of us. "Who knew you could clean up so well."

"I'm always handsome," he replies.

"Debatable," she teases him.

Thankfully, Zoey has not fallen for my brother, but since the shit with Mark, she hasn't bothered to fall for anyone else either.

"You're a stunner," he tells her.

"Sharla," Zoey shoots back. "Don't be an asshole. I like her."

"Me too," he tells her.

"Then tell her she's a stunner."

"Sharla knows she's a stunner."

"So do I," Zoey says, putting him in his place. "Women don't need their egos stroked as often as men."

My brother laughs as he walks beside her. Our maid of honor and best man. They're the two most important people in our lives, besides each other.

I've grown closer to Liam over the last year, closer than we've been since we were little kids. He isn't a bad guy. Sure, he is still a jagoff, but he has his moments of kindness, even if they are as rare as spotting a black Florida panther in the wild.

Lulu chuckles beside me, squeezing my hand. "They fight like they're siblings," she says, peering up at me and squinting from the fading sunlight.

"That they do," I tell her.

The night passes quickly.

Dinner. Drinks. Dancing.

The sun slowly drops below the horizon as the lights on the terrace kick on, casting the party in a soft glow.

We've spoken to every single person who's attended the wedding, and that took most of our time.

Lulu's family is mind-bogglingly large, and I won't remember half their names by morning.

"This was the best day ever," Lulu says in my arms as we move around the dance floor.

"Mine too, sweetheart," I say, adjusting my arm around her waist and holding her closer.

"It's time for the bouquet," the DJ says into the microphone.

"I have to," Lulu tells me as she pushes out of my arms. "It's almost time for us to leave."

Thank God.

"All the single ladies to the dance floor," the man says, and no fewer than twenty women make their way to the middle, huddling together.

I watch as my wife climbs up near the DJ booth, waving to her friends and family who are waiting to catch the bouquet, a tradition I've never really understood.

Zoey stands in the dead center, looking about as uninterested as I feel. Lulu turns around and lifts her arms a few times before she lets go, and the bouquet of flowers hurtles through the air.

I watch in amazement as the women lunge forward, misjudging the distance, and completely miss the catch. But the flowers smack Zoey right in the chest and drop into her hands.

"Fuck," she mutters, staring down at the flowers like they're about to catch fire.

Lulu turns, her eyes widening when she realizes

her sister caught the bouquet. "Yay," she says, clapping.

"Damn it," Zoey groans as she marches toward Lulu. "You did that on purpose."

"My aim isn't that good, sissy."

"You turned into a professional thrower."

"There's no such thing as a professional thrower."

"Like Uncle Vinnie."

"He was a quarterback."

"Whatever." Zoey rolls her eyes, trying to give the flowers back to Lulu.

Lulu pushes them back into Zoey's chest. "Someday you'll think different, and you'll find yourself an Oliver."

My eyebrows rise. "I'm a thing now?" I ask, marching up to my wife and her sister.

"Not all men are like you," Zoey says, turning her gaze toward my dipshit brother. "They're like him."

"I can't argue with you there," I tell her, laughing as my brother hits on every single woman at the party but is immediately shot down. "He's making his rounds."

"And not winning a damn thing," Lulu says, watching Liam. "Thank God the women in my family have common sense."

"Can we go now?" I ask Lulu.

Zoey giggles. "Someone wants to get lucky." She nudges her shoulder into mine, looking genuinely happy for the first time in a long while.

"I already got lucky. Your sister said yes," I explain to her.

"We can go," Lulu says to me, taking my arm. "I need to get off my feet."

"That's the plan," I tell her with a wink.

"I don't need to hear this," Zoey says, covering her ears. "It's too much, even for me."

"I'm ready to start our forever."

"I thought we already did," Lulu says, and she's right.

Our forever started the moment we met, but neither of us knew it.

CHAPTER 23
LULU

"MAY I CUT IN?" my father asks Oliver.

"Of course." Oliver gives my father my hand and steps backward to where my mother's waiting to scoop him up.

"Daddy," I whisper, placing my hand in his and resting the other one on his shoulder.

"I remember you standing on my shoes, dancing like this," he sighs and gazes down into my eyes. "It feels like yesterday."

"Time moves quickly."

"Too quickly," he says. "It's been hard for me to let go."

"You don't say." I smile up at the man who raised me to be the person I am today. Not a day went by that I didn't feel loved and wanted by him, even if he isn't my biological father.

"I think I did well."

"You did, Dad. Better than I thought you would."

"Someday, you'll have kids, and you'll understand the overwhelming need to protect them. But there were times you and your sister didn't make it easy on us."

I giggle, thinking of all the dumb shit we did growing up. Most of it, my parents don't know about —and never will, if we can help it. "It kept you young."

"Do you see the wrinkles on my face? My two girls put them there."

"Daddy, I think a few are from Mom too."

"A few, but I wouldn't have it any other way, Lulu. You and Zoey are my greatest joys."

"You're going to make me cry," I whisper, wrinkling my nose as my vision starts to blur.

"Do a favor for this old man?"

"You're not old."

He stares at me. "I am, kiddo, and I'm not getting any younger."

"Okay."

"Live a life you're proud of. Be happy. Never settle for anything less."

"I am happy."

He kisses my cheek tenderly. "Your mom and I only want the best for you."

"I love you, Dad."

"I love you too."

My gaze lands on my sister. She's sitting at a table with our younger cousins. "Do you think Zoey's going to be able to find love?"

"She will. It may be a while, but someone will come along and sweep her off her feet."

"She's not going to make it easy."

"There's a man out there strong enough for her."

"I hope so," I say as I lean forward, placing my head on his shoulder. "She deserves the love and happiness I found."

"Everyone does," he replies, holding me tighter. "I didn't think I'd find it, but your mom showed up out of nowhere, and I knew my life would never be the same."

"You loved me first, didn't you?"

"You stole my heart, kiddo. You were instantly my best friend."

I smile against his shoulder, remembering all the photos of us when I was little. "Still am."

"Your mom might argue with you about that."

I chuckle. "We don't have to tell her."

I don't know what I did to get so lucky. The day my mom walked into the Hook & Hustle, everything changed for us. At the time, my mom thought our world was ending, but the best part of her life was about to begin.

Our lives would've been so very different if my grandfather hadn't disowned her. I wouldn't have the

Gallos, my father, and Zoey would've never been born.

I can't imagine that world. My life has been so full because of my family, and no one has been as lucky as I am to be surrounded by so many people who love me.

EPILOGUE
LULU

OLIVER LOOKS SHELL-SHOCKED.

"You okay?" I ask, grabbing his hand.

"We have a kid," he whispers, staring down at our baby in my arms.

"We do."

"We have a girl," he adds.

"We do." I squeeze his hand.

"We made a human."

"I know. Isn't it amazing?"

"I've never been more scared in my entire life, and that's saying something because I've been through some crazy shit," he whispers.

I chuckle as I look at the totally rattled hulk of a man. "It'll be fine."

"Someone's going to hurt her someday, and I'm going to have to murder him and then spend the rest of my life in jail. You'll be alone. She'll be alone. I'll miss everything."

"Baby." I can't hide my smile. "That's not going to happen."

"Men are shitheads. It'll happen." He reaches for the baby, and I give her over willingly. "Hey, baby girl."

I thought my husband was sexy before, but nothing beats seeing him holding our child. She's a tiny thing, but she looks like a peanut in his arms.

He palms her head, laying her body down the inside of his arm. "We need to talk, kid," he says, looking so damn serious. "I'm your daddy, and I'm the one who's going to protect you from the world."

"Don't scare her already."

"She needs to be prepared."

"She's an hour old."

"No time like the present."

I drop my head back onto the pillow and smile. "Whatever you say, sweetheart."

"You're learning," he says to me before he gives his undivided attention back to our new baby. "Now, where was I?" He sits on the edge of the bed, resting one hand on my leg while he holds our little girl. "I want you to be a book girl. You're going to stay home and read instead of going out with boys."

"Baby," I say, shaking my head. "You can't tell her that. It doesn't work that way."

"It will." He looks so sure of himself. He is in for a

world of hurt, but it is something he'll have to find out on his own.

If our daughter is anything like me or Zoey, he is going to have a very stressful few decades.

"I'll build you a library."

"Stop it, Oliver. I want her to have so many friends."

"Only girls."

"All kids."

"No," he says, his gaze moving to me for a moment. "Boys are off-limits until she's thirty."

"Ridiculous," I mutter. "You're going to be a problem."

"Daddy's not the problem. Other boys are."

I roll my eyes. "She'll have to kiss a few frogs to find her prince."

"No. No frogs for you."

"This should be fun."

There's a knock on the door before my mom pops her head into the room. "You're awake?"

"Yeah." I motion for her to come in. She was in the delivery room with us, and so was Zoey. I drew the line when it came to my dad, and he was okay with it. I guess he almost fainted when Zoey was born. The big guy couldn't handle seeing my mother in pain, but I think it was more about the blood, although he'd never admit it.

She pushes open the door and is followed into the room by my father. "We brought you a soda."

I hold out my hands and wiggle my fingers. "I'm so thirsty."

"Is that healthy?" Oliver asks, and I pin him with a glare that makes him seal his lips shut.

"It's best not to talk," Dad says to Oliver, having been in his shoes a very long time ago. "You won't win."

"Never do," Oliver mumbles, but he hasn't taken his eyes off our baby. The man is mesmerized.

"Do we have a name yet?" Mom asks, standing in front of Oliver and staring at her first grandbaby.

"I think so," I tell her.

"And?" she says.

"Harlow," I reply.

"Harlow?" She tilts her head as her eyes roam the little girl's face. "Does she look like an Harlow?"

"She looks like an overripe prune," Dad says.

"Harlow Rose," Oliver says. "It's perfect for her."

"May I?" Mom opens her hands, wanting the baby.

The kid's feet will probably barely touch the ground until she's able to run a marathon. Babies are popular in this family, and I already know people will be fighting over holding her.

"Support her head," Oliver tells my mom, like she's new to the baby business.

"Oli, I think I know what I'm doing," she says and laughs. "I've got this. Relax."

"I'm strung so tight right now."

Dad slaps Oliver's shoulder. "You'll be that way the rest of your life. Settle into it. It's the new you."

"What?" Oliver asks, his eyes wide as he looks at my dad. "You're lying."

"It's the truth. You'll never know another day's peace until you're buried in the ground."

Mom slaps Dad on the chest with the back of her hand. "Don't scare him."

"Have you ever been relaxed in thirty years, Delilah?" he asks her, crossing his arms over his chest.

"Well…no."

"See?" Dad pitches a thumb at Mom as he tilts his head. "No peace."

"Damn it," Oliver mutters.

"I brought cheesecake," Zoey says, coming into the room in a mad rush. "I went to Eli's."

My eyes widen as they land on the bag she's carrying from my favorite cheesecake place in the city. "You're the best sister in the world."

"Godmother worthy?" she asks, holding the bag out of reach and raising an eyebrow.

"You're going to bribe me with food?"

She nods. "Is it working?"

"You got the job."

She fist-pumps the air in triumph. "Worth every bit of traffic."

I snatch the bag from her hands before she has a chance to hold the dessert ransom for any other reason. "I still think it's ridiculous Grandma wouldn't let me have this while I was pregnant. Cheesecake is safe."

"You know how she is," Dad says, placing his hand on my blanket-covered leg. "She is overprotective."

"My body needs this to survive," I say as I open the first container, salivating the moment the smell of the turtle cheesecake hits me.

"You're always so dramatic," Mom says.

I point at my sister with the plastic spoon. "Have you met Zoey? She's all drama, all the time."

"Hey." Zoey makes a move like she's about to steal the bag away, but even in my tired state, I'm too fast for her.

"No. It's mine."

"Always greedy," she whispers.

"This is the life," Dad says, ignoring our bickering. "I'm a grandpa."

"I don't feel like a granny," Mom says.

"You don't look like one either," Dad says to her, his gaze traveling a little too slowly up her body.

"I'm trying to eat," I tell him, digging into the cheesecake like I've never eaten before.

"You want to share that?" Oliver asks, reaching out like he's going to take my spoon, but he thinks better of it when I glare at him. "Guess not."

"You can have the plain one in the bag."

"Better than nothing," he says and pulls out the

slice of plain cheesecake, which I am more than happy to sacrifice because it is my least favorite.

"Sorry we're late. Your grandfather is a…" Grandma says as she walks into the room, but her words die as soon as her eyes land on the baby. "I forgot how little they are when they're born."

"You had four of us," Dad says.

"It was a wild time in our lives, honey, and I'm old. My memory isn't as good as it used to be."

Grandma peeks over Mom's shoulder. "She's perfect."

"She is," Mom says.

"Do we have a name?" Grandpa asks.

"Harlow Rose," I tell him between cheesecake bites.

"Welcome to the world, Harlow Rose," Grandma says to our little girl. "I can't wait to spoil you rotten."

I watch my family, the people who raised me, knowing that I have the luckiest child in the world. She will never know loneliness with the Gallos in her life. She'd also never know peace and privacy either. That is the trade-off, but it's totally worth it.

Oliver slides onto the bed next to me. "They're happy."

"There's a baby," I tell him. "That always makes them happy."

"I'm happy too," he replies.

I glance at him and smile. "I don't know if I've ever been this happy before."

He lifts his hand and wipes the corner of my mouth with his fingertip. "How long do we have to be here?"

"I think they'll let us go before dinner."

"Good. I want to get home and start the rest of our life."

I like the sound of that. Everything shifted the day I met Oliver, and I wouldn't change a thing, not even losing my car. All of it led to this moment in time, surrounded by my family, husband, and new baby.

I am the luckiest woman in the world, and I won't take a moment of it for granted.

Ready for more Sinners? Zoey Gallo's story is next!
>> visit menofinked.com/wish to grab your copy

New to the Gallos? Start at the beginning of the family saga with Throttle Me, Men of Inked Book >> visit menofinked.com/throttle-me to download

♥ Men of Inked Reader Guide ♥

Visit **menofinked.com/guide** to download the Men of Inked Reader Guide, which includes a family tree, printable reading guide, and information about each Gallo family saga read.

New MC Series - Hot Biker Alert!

Johnny "Shadow" Butch isn't the type to mingle with people outside his world unless they owe him or the club something. But when his eyes land on a beautiful woman in need of a place to stay, he offers her shelter from the coming storm without a second thought.

Violet James needed a fresh start. She's planned every detail—new job, new house, new city. But the one thing she didn't expect was a hurricane to throw a wrench into everything. Stranded in a new city with no open hotel rooms for miles, she's intrigued when a handsome biker offers her a safe place to stay.

Shadow never expected the woman to come with baggage in the form of an obsessive ex-boyfriend who will stop at nothing to get her back, including showing up at his club's compound.

What starts off as a little fun to pass the time as a hurricane decimates the area around them turns into something deeper than either of them could've imagined. And Shadow will do anything to keep Violet safe, even if that means risking his life to save hers.

>> *visit __menofinked.com/shadow__ to download*

To purchase signed paperbacks and more, please visit
chelleblissromance.com

ABOUT THE AUTHOR

I'm a full-time writer, time-waster extraordinaire, social media addict, coffee fiend, and ex-history teacher. *To learn more about my books, please visit menofinked.com.*

Want to stay up-to-date on the newest Men of Inked release and more? Tap here to join my newsletter or visit *menofinked.com/inked-news*

Join over 10,000 readers on Facebook in Chelle Bliss Books private reader group and talk books and all things reading. Tap here to become part of the family or visit at *facebook.com/groups/blisshangout*

Tap here to see the Gallo Family Tree or visit *menofinked.com/gallo-family-tree*

Where to Follow Me: